The Little One's Christmas Dream

IRIS COLE

Disclaimer

This story is a work of fiction, any resemblance to people is purely coincidence. All places, names, events, businesses, etc. are used in a fictional manner. All characters are from the imagination of the author.

Would you like a free book?

CLAIM

THE FOUNDLING BABY

HERE

https://dl.bookfunnel.com/kji81fn0dr

Table of Contents

Chapter One

The snowflakes drifted over the cobbled square, slow and shining in the glow of the lamppost on the corner. Betty stretched out a small, fat hand, the fingertips nipped blue with cold. A snowflake settled on her pink palm. She held it up, admiring it for the few seconds it remained on her skin: its jagged edges, the perfectly unique construction of its fluffy surface. Then it melted away, a pinprick of cold against her hand, and Betty giggled.

"Miss Parker!" she said. "Look!"

There was no response. Betty raised her head, then remembered that Miss Parker had said that she was going to be a few minutes. She'd gone into the shop nearby, the one with all the colourful bunting in the window and the pretty green Christmas tree just behind the glass. The tree was all draped in satiny ribbons, yellow and red and blue, and it had a big golden star right at the very top. Betty wondered who had put that star up there. They had an even bigger tree at home, and Mama had had to pick Betty up above her head to put their decoration on top of their tree. It wasn't a star, though.

It was an angel at Betty's house; Mama always said that it was far too easy to forget that Christmas was really about angels and guiding stars and the beauty of a Babe in a manger. Betty didn't really know what that meant, but she liked angels.

She rubbed her hands against each other to keep them warm and squinted past the tree into the shop to see if Miss Parker was nearly done.

She'd gone inside to buy some string for cook's Christmas pudding and some pearl drops. Betty's mouth watered at the thought of the Christmas day treats. The pudding was not her favourite, but it didn't, matter she was sure to have a bowl of custard just for herself.

Mama said she could. She wasn't sure how long a few minutes were, but it had still been light when Miss Parker went into the shop, and now twilight settled icily over the bustling square. A few minutes must be almost up.

She couldn't see all the way into the sweet shop, but she had a good view of the counter. It was all decked out with holly and pretty displays of toffees and biscuits and that fancy new chocolate that came in solid bars that Mama loved to buy her. The proprietor moved past the counter, sweeping the floor.

Miss Parker would go up to him to pay any minute now, Betty guessed. Then they would go home to a hot fire and dinner, and bath time and story time. And Mama would kiss her and put her to bed.

Betty giggled. Then it would be one less sleep until Christmas, and Miss Parker had shown her on her fingers that Christmas was not very far away.

She wrapped her arms around herself and rocked back and forth on her heels, humming. Today had already been so exciting. They'd come to the square after playtime in the park that afternoon, before it had begun to snow; now the pointed rooftops were all draped in a pale, glimmering blanket, and every cobblestone was outlined in white snow.

Miss Parker had taken Betty into the strangest shop she had ever seen. It was tucked away on the edge of this square—which was much smaller than the one where they usually went shopping—and all the clothes were colourless and ugly. Miss Parker had bought Betty the dress she was wearing right now. They were going to dress up as street urchins, Miss Parker said, just to play pretend. Betty loved to play pretend and she loved to try on dresses. She looked at herself in the reflection of the sweet-shop window now and grinned, tangling her small hands in her dress, then lifting it up to fan out the skirt. It was a plain grey thing, slightly itchy, and it didn't flare out from her waist the way her other dress did. It was so different and interesting.

Still, she hoped Miss Parker would come out soon. This dress's fabric was scratchy and thick, but it was only a single layer. Now that the sun had set, Betty longed for her thick wool dress and her warm, fleece-lined coat. Those were back in the shop, where Miss Parker had given them to the man behind the counter. For safekeeping, she said.

Betty licked her lips. Maybe Miss Parker would bring a chocolate bar, too, for a snack on the way home. She was starving.

The bell on the church tower at the edge of the square tolled quietly, the sound muffled behind the tumbling flakes. Betty tried to count the rings. One, two, three, four... She wasn't that good at counting yet, and the numbers jumbled up and fell away.

Footsteps inside the sweet shop made her jump. She turned to the door, smiling, ready for Miss Parker to come out and take her home, but there was no sign of her governess. Instead, it was the shop's proprietor, broom still in hand.

3

He flipped the sign over on the door. Then he took a key out of his pocket to lock up.

"Sir!" Betty cried. She ran to him, wincing as her bare feet stuck to the snowy cobbles. "Sir, wait!"

The proprietor stopped, his eyes narrowing at the sight of Betty. "What do you want?"

"Miss Parker is in there," said Betty. "My gov'ness."

The proprietor laughed. "Try your tricks elsewhere, child. There's nobody in here." He locked the door with a click.

"Sir, wait!" Betty cried, but the man had already turned away.

He must have made a mistake. Miss Parker was in there, behind one of the shelves or some such. But from this angle, Betty could see the whole of the sweet shop, with all its polished glass and bright displays, and she saw for sure that there was no sign of Miss Parker.

The truth pierced her like an icicle to the chest. Miss Parker was gone.

"Miss Parker?" Betty cried.

She spun around. The square yawned around her, huge and grim and cold. It seemed to grow bigger as she watched, the building leaning inward, ready to collapse on her, to consume her.

Betty screamed, "Miss Parker!" as loudly as she could, her voice trailing off into a desperate wheeze. She was crying now, tears rolling down her cheeks. Miss Parker had told her to stay where she was, but Betty was too scared now; she ran across the square and screamed her governess's name again and again. She stared into every window, hammered on the door of every shop, but most of them were empty. Everyone in the world had gone home, it seemed. Everyone except Betty.

"Miss Parker!" Betty shrieked.

Her screams echoed and echoed around the square, and the snow was falling faster now, and it was absolutely dark and absolutely cold. She hugged herself, shivering and sobbing, and she screamed until a woman on the corner said, "There! There she is."

Betty whirled around, looking, but there was no sign of Miss Parker.

She turned back to the woman, a young woman who pushed a cart full of oranges. She had been selling them earlier; Miss Parker had bought one for herself, and promised to buy one for Betty later. They were fat and round and golden, spots of colour in the grey, black and white of the square.

Next to the woman, a big man in a black uniform frowned at Betty. His long black hat had a silver shield on it. "What about her?"

"Well, she's lost, isn't she?" said the young woman. "She's running around calling out for someone, and I've been watching her all afternoon. She's just been there on the corner, waiting, and nobody's come for her."

Betty screwed her fists into her eyes and sobbed, so cold and hungry and afraid that she barely understood the young woman's words.

"What do you want me to do about it?" said the man.

"Well, you should find her parents, shouldn't you? They must be looking for her. Look at her hair—it's been washed and combed, and her cheeks are so rosy. Someone has been caring for her."

The man laughed. "Look at her dress, girl. She's just another urchin trying her luck. Nobody's looking for her."

He walked away, and Betty sank down in the snow and pulled her knees to her chest. She had ended up underneath the lamppost again, and its stone footing gave her a little shelter from the wind.

The young woman stared at her for a few moments more. Then she pushed her cart and hurried away, and Betty was alone in the cold and the snow. She curled up against the lamppost, closed her eyes, and cried until she fell asleep.

~ ~ ~ ~ ~

Martha Evans hummed to herself as she strolled down the pavement, her sensible shoes crunching in the fresh layer of pure white snow that had fallen overnight. It was barely touched by traffic this early in the morning; Martha liked to get her shopping done before the crowds started, when everything was still crisp and fresh.

Christmas was just two days away, and Martha's shopping list was a long one, but she couldn't help smiling as she strolled past the little church at the edge of the square. The children's choir was practicing inside. Their pure, high voices were muffled through the stone walls, but Martha could still make out the words of "Angels We Have Heard on High", and she hummed along as she walked into the square.

At this time of morning, only a few harried-looking mothers and hungry men browsed the small shops that lined the cobbled space. Martha avoided a seedy character with yellow teeth and long, dirty nails, then headed for the grocer's, her first stop. The jovial man behind the counter was whistling as he set greenhouse tomatoes, slightly wrinkled potatoes, and fat round turnips on display.

Martha pushed the door open. "Good morning, Mr. Potts!"

The old man looked up and chuckled toothily. "Good morning, Mrs. Evans! Lovely to see you. Are you shopping for the mistress again today?"

"That's right," said Martha.

Mr. Potts shook his head. "Funny old bird, ain't she? Letting you shop with the poor folk, like. Not every mistress would accept cabbages and flour and fruit from the likes of us."

"She always says that it's foolish to spend extra money just because something comes from a more fashionable square," said Martha.

Mr. Potts chuckled. "Like I said. A funny old bird."

"You're not wrong, Mr. Potts. Not wrong at all." Martha smiled. "But a *good* old bird, nonetheless."

"You speak the truth, Mrs. Evans, and there ain't very many of them living in that part of town, is there?"

"Not at all," said Martha.

"What can I get you?" asked Mrs. Potts.

Martha pushed the list over the counter to him and set her basket beside it, and he shuffled around, selecting potatoes and onions and a fat pumpkin for his favourite customer. Martha gazed around the little shop, admiring the ribbons in the corners, the gingerbread men hanging from the ceiling.

"Mrs. Potts has done a wonderful job decorating this year," she said.

"Oh yes, she always loves it. She's out shopping for ribbon to make a wreath for the front door," said Mr. Potts. "Busy time of year for folk like us, but somehow my Evelyn always makes it a beautiful time, too."

"That's a gift, make no mistake," said Martha.

The square was poor, but only the ugly slop-shop in the corner was unadorned. Looking through the window, Martha admired the colourful bunting in the sweet shop's window, the bright candles burning in the window of the pawn shop.

Something caught her eye near the sweet shop. Martha frowned. A tiny figure was huddled underneath the lamppost

7

on the corner; a little girl in a shapeless grey dress, her cheeks nipped red with cold. Her eyes were closed, and Martha would have thought that she was dead already if she hadn't been slowly rubbing her small hands together as if to keep them warm.

"Who's that, Mr. Potts?" Martha asked. "She doesn't look like any of the urchins around here."

"Doesn't look like any urchin at all, you ask me," said Mr. Potts.

"How's that?"

"Well, if you get closer, you'll see. Round rosy cheeks. Not missing any fingers or toes—yet." Mr. Potts shrugged. "I'd say she's been abandoned. Another family with nothing to eat for Christmas, perhaps."

Sadness curled in Martha's heart. "I don't know how anyone can do that to a child. What I wouldn't give—" She stopped short and pressed a hand to her belly, trying not to think of the quiet parade of children who had grown and blossomed there and yet somehow withered and died before their nine months were up.

"Evelyn went to speak to her, but the poor mite's so afraid, she nearly ran into that alley. You know the one. Where the men with the opium go. We thought it best to leave her," said Mr. Potts.

"Perhaps," said Martha, "but—perhaps I'll speak to her."

"You could try." Mr. Potts shrugged. "Poor wretch won't last long out there. You always did have a way with children."

Martha was counting on it. She spotted a red apple on the shelf nearby and said, "Would you add this to my bill please, Mr. Potts?"

The grocer agreed, and Martha took the apple and left the shop. The bright white snow creaked as she walked across the bonny little square, and the nearer she drew to the child, the more she saw that Mr. Potts was right. This was no urchin. Her cheeks were chapped with cold, but they were plump and pink; her dress was poor now, but the curls that spilled over it were the richest shade of brown that Martha had ever seen, like chocolate made just right. The girl's eyes were closed, her lashes flecked with ice, and she rubbed her small hands together in a tiny motion that had allowed her fingertips to turn blue, but not black.

Martha stopped a few feet away. "Hello, pet," she said softly.

The little girl opened her eyes, a startling shade of green, and stared at her.

Martha crouched and held out the apple. "Aren't you hungry?"

A small gasp escaped the girl. She extended her hands toward the apple, and Martha held it closer to her chest, then reached out. "Why don't you come with me into the warm," she said, "and then we can have an apple?"

The child stared into her eyes. She looked bitterly afraid; her eyelids were scarlet with weeping, and tears had washed two clean trails on her grubby cheeks.

"It's all right," said Martha. "It's quite safe."

Something about her voice convinced the little girl to trust her. She took Martha's hand, her tiny fingers very cold in Martha's palm, and Martha handed her the apple. The girl bit into it and crunched it in hungry, panting bites.

"Come on, pet," said Martha, gently closing her fingers over the little girl's hand. "Let's go inside."

Still eating, the child allowed herself to be led across the square to the grocer's shop. Mr. Potts shook his head, waving his hands behind the window in his door, but Martha ignored him. She pushed the door open and led the child into the blissful warmth of the shop, which had a fire crackling behind the counter.

"There you are." Martha sat her down in a corner. "Eat your apple and warm yourself, there's a good girl."

"What are you doing?" Mr. Potts hissed. "You can't bring her in here!"

"Don't worry, Mr. Potts," said Martha. "I'm only letting her eat something and get warm."

Mr. Potts frowned. "Only to turn her back out into the cold?"

"Of course not." Martha smiled and ran a hand over the child's dark hair. "You say you believe she was abandoned?"

"I do," said Mr. Potts. "At any rate, no one's been here looking for her."

"If anyone does," said Martha, "will you tell me?"

Mr. Potts frowned. "Of course, but Martha, what are you thinking?"

Martha gazed at the child for a long few moments before she answered. "I'm thinking, Mr. Potts, that I am a lonely old widow, that my womb never bore any fruit, and that my husband has been gone for much too long. I've had enough of being alone. This little girl needs somewhere to go, and she can go with me."

Mr. Potts stared at her. "What about Mrs. Bromley?"

"My mistress is kind-hearted, as you said," said Martha.

Mr. Potts laughed. "Oh, Mrs. Evans, *no* rich folk are kind-hearted enough to take in a child like that. Or even to allow their cook to take in a child like that."

"Perhaps," said Martha. "But perhaps not. I will throw those dice, Mr. Potts, for the sake of a child like that."

The little girl had finished her apple, leaving the core; another sign that this was no urchin. She held out the core and said politely, "Where may I throw this away?"

"You can give it to me, dear." Martha took it. "Do you feel better?"

The girl nodded.

"What's your name, darling?" Martha asked.

"Betty," the girl whispered.

"Well then, Betty." Martha held out a hand. "Why don't you come with me, and we'll get you a real breakfast?"

When the child's eyes lit up, they filled Martha's world with light.

~ ~ ~ ~ ~

The man in the grocer's shop had called the lady Mrs. Evans, but she had said to Betty that she should call her Martha. Martha had nice wide hips that wiggled when she walked, and her hand was soft, warm and squishy as she held Betty's. It was very different from Miss Parker's hands, which were always cold and hard. After the terrible cold, which had made everything hurt so much, Martha's hand felt like heaven. The grocer's shop felt like heaven too.

Martha gave her bread and cheese and another apple and Betty ate and ate, huddled next to the fire. Martha and her friend, a nice old man, kept asking Betty where she lived or what her parents' names were. Betty didn't know her parents' names or where her house was. She only knew that Miss Parker had sold her dress and left her in the snow, and after a long while spent talking quietly behind the counter with her friend, Martha came and took Betty's hand and said, "How would you

11

like to come home with me? There's plenty of food and warmth, and love, too," and so of course Betty said yes.

She knew that she would go home to Mama, of course. Martha must be Betty's new gov'ness, like Miss Parker. She'd had many governesses and Miss Parker was not a very nice one. She would much rather have Martha, and she skipped along beside her as they walked through the crisp, wintry morning. A little robin, a splash of bright colour against the snow, perched on a fence nearby and sang his tiny heart out. There were big yellow ribbons on the palisades in front of many of the big houses on this road, and Christmas trees on the smooth white lawns, and the jingle of harness bells sounded as fine horses in carriages with their doors hung with wreaths came trotting past. Martha always pulled Betty a little closer, well out of the way of the carriages. Miss Parker had never done any such thing.

"It's going to be such a nice Christmas," said Betty.

Martha squeezed her hand. "Yes," she murmured. "Yes, you know, I think it is."

~ ~ ~ ~ ~

Adelaide Bromley had her back to the door when Martha came in. The old lady was elegantly arrayed on her settee, a tray of morning tea by her elbow. The housemaid had drawn back the thick red drapes on the huge window, letting in a pool of crisp wintry sunlight and offering a view of the garden Adelaide loved so much. Holly bushes lined one side, their berries as bright as jewels, and a row of pine trees shielded the house from the road. They were dusted with snow now, thick and fine as icing sugar on a Christmas cake.

"Good morning, Mrs. Bromley," said Martha.

"Martha, Martha, do come in!" said Adelaide, gesturing sweepingly with one arm. "Come and look at the holly bushes! Aren't they bright this morning?"

Martha entered the room and curtseyed to Mrs. Bromley.

"Please sit, dear," said Adelaide. "You must be tired after your walk to the market. Did you find everything you needed?"

It had taken years for Martha to grow comfortable enough to sit in Adelaide's presence, but she perched carefully now on the edge of an armchair. "Yes, thank you, ma'am." She smiled. "I really think I did, this time."

Adelaide lowered her delicate china teacup into its saucer. "Why, Martha, you have such a strange look in your eye. Happy, yet a little frightened." She laughed. "If I didn't know any better, I'd say you were in love."

"Perhaps I am, in a way," said Martha. Desperation made her reckless. "Mrs. Bromley, there's something I must ask you."

Adelaide set her teacup aside. "Anything, my dear. Please. Go on."

Martha took a deep breath and looked around the house, scraping together her courage. Her eyes rested on the Christmas tree that had been set up in the corner for more than a week. It was all hung with oranges and baubles and ribbons, and a glittering white angel with real feathers for its wings perched on the very top, ready for Adelaide's grandchildren to arrive later that day.

The sight of the angel gave Martha courage.

"Mrs. Bromley," she said, "I found a little girl on the street, and I wanted to know if I might keep her and raise her as my own."

Adelaide's eyes widened. "A little girl—! How?"

Martha told her about how she'd found the child huddled under the lamppost, and how she'd questioned her at length.

13

"It seems as though her father has taken a new wife—the girl calls her Miss Parker," said Martha. "I believe the stepmother must have abandoned her. The man at the slop shop confirmed it. He showed me the loveliest little cotton dress and said that a woman with the girl had sold it to him, and bought a cheap, ugly dress for the child."

"The poor mite!" said Adelaide. "You must be right, Martha. She *has* been abandoned." Adelaide sighed. "A poor little scrap like that with nowhere else to go."

The truth that Adelaide didn't know was that a child, such as Betty, had many other places to go, Martha thought. Places like the cotton mills and the match factories, the workhouses and the streets, places where beautiful, gentle children like Betty were churned up and killed.

"I know that it's a little strange," said Martha softly. "But she'll pull her weight, ma'am. She can learn to do little things now, and in a few years she'll be the finest scullery-maid you ever saw in your life. She won't eat much. She can eat from my rations. You won't have to worry about her at all; she can sleep in my room, and—"

"Oh, Martha." Adelaide rose to her feet and grasped Martha's hands in both of hers; they were so soft, and very warm. "Sweet Martha, you forget how long you've been with me. I've seen you try again and again to bear a little child of your own, and I've seen you lose your dear husband. How could I deny a dear child that God has brought you for a Christmas gift?"

Tears filled Martha's eyes. "Thank you, Mrs. Bromley."

"I know she will be an asset to this house, because you will raise her that way." Adelaide smiled. "Now, if I am not mistaken, dear Martha, it is about time for breakfast—and I'm sure your little one would like some, too."

Your little one. The words sent tendrils of warmth deep into Martha's soul. She curtseyed and made for the door, but paused by the Christmas tree to gaze up at the gauzy white angel at the top.

"Thank you," she mouthed.

Chapter Two

It seemed like Betty had barely closed her eyes when a gentle hand was on her shoulder.

"Wake up, darling Little One," said Martha. "It's time to get to work."

Betty opened her eyes, even though her eyelids felt like sandpaper against them. She blinked up at a bare wooden ceiling, so different from the ceiling in her nursery at home, with its pretty trim and cheerful wallpaper. This ceiling was as simple and matter-of-fact as the bare white walls of the small room she'd shared with Martha last night.

She sat up on the pile of blankets that had been put in the corner for her. Martha had said she would have a bed soon, but last night she hadn't minded at all; she had slept in the same cot her entire life, and the blankets were warm and cosy enough, and it all felt like a grand adventure. But now, with the cold morning air seeping through the floorboards, and the dismal sound of a draft howling unfamiliarly around the eaves of the big house, Betty suddenly felt that she would give anything for her same old cot and her cheerful wallpaper and her trimmed ceiling and Mama's sweet voice singing her a lullaby.

"Why is it so dark?" Betty asked. "Is it the middle of the night?"

"No, darling." Martha chuckled. "It's five in the morning. Time to start the day. Come along—I'll give you some milk and bread in the kitchen."

Betty had never been in a kitchen before yesterday, when Martha had given her breakfast. It was a marvellous place with big ovens and strings of onions hanging from the ceiling and the smell of dried herbs everywhere. Now, though, when Martha led her inside, it was bitterly cold and felt so dark. There was nothing but darkness through the mesh curtains on the windows, and the gas lamp's light was both brutal and insufficient. A little girl crouched near the fireplace, wearing a black-and-white uniform. She added wood to the fire and prodded it with a cast-iron poker.

"Soon be warm as you like," said Martha. "Bring me a cup and plate from the scullery, there's a darling."

Rubbing her eyes and yawning, Betty stumbled over to the scullery, a big, bare, cold room containing little more than two giant sinks and a cabinet full of cutlery and crockery. She picked out a nice china cup and a matching little plate and toddled into the kitchen with them. When the girl by the fire saw her, her eyes turned wide.

"Mrs. Evans!" she cried.

Martha, who stood by the pantry door, turned around sharply. "Oh, no darling!" she said sharply, grabbing the cup and plate from Betty's hands. "These are not ours. These are only for the mistress and her family and guests. We don't use these."

Betty blinked, startled. "Why not? They're so pretty."

"Because they are not ours," Martha snapped. "You will never touch these again unless you are going to clean them. Do you understand?"

Her voice was so hard and sharp that it scared Betty. She swallowed hard, but couldn't keep the tears from spilling down her cheeks. "I'm sorry," she sobbed out. "I'm sorry."

"Don't cry. It's all right." Martha patted her head as she walked by to put the cup and plate away. "You weren't to know."

Betty still struggled to swallow her tears as Martha selected a tin cup and plate instead. They were so ugly and plain, but Betty dared not say anything. Martha cut three hefty slices of bread, buttered them, and set them out on three of the ugly plates. She poured tea for herself and the girl, milk for Betty, watered down slightly.

"Here. Eat up quickly," said Martha, lifting Betty onto a chair by the table.

Betty shook her head. "I'm not hungry. It's like night time."

"Well, you'll eat it up and be grateful for it," said Martha, "for you'll need it later in the morning. It's Christmas Eve, the longest day of the year. We have plenty of work to do."

Betty didn't understand. Christmas Eve was hardly a time for work. It was a time when she sat at the table with Mama and Papa like a grown-up, and got to eat roast goose and mince pies and the wonderful mint sauce that always arrived on the table at Christmas. It was a time for presents, oranges, sweets and laughter, for tiny sips of eggnog stolen from Mama's cup, and Papa playing the piano and singing until everyone clapped except for Mama.

The tears filled her eyes as she bit into her bread.

"Dry your eyes, Little One," said Martha. "There's nothing to be done about it now."

In seconds, Martha and the girl—her name was Verity—had finished their bread. Betty gulped the last of her milk with the best will she could muster.

"Right. Verity, knead the breakfast dough," Martha ordered. "We'll give Mrs. Bromley tea and biscuits early, so that we can have a lovely spread waiting for the family. I'll arrange that, and then we need to get to work on the kippers, the bacon, the beans and the eggs. Betty, you shall learn how to wash the dishes as we go."

Half an hour later, standing on a stool that Martha fetched for her, Betty's hands were plunged into lukewarm soapy water. She clutched a sponge and worked it across the surface of the tin plate she'd just used. The sponge was slippery in her small fingers, and her hands felt uncoordinated and stupid.

A cup slipped from her fingers and plopped into the water.

"Mrs. Evans!" Verity shrieked. "She's dropping things."

The tone of her voice made Betty jump, and tears instantly filled her eyes.

"What did she drop?" Martha shouted from the kitchen, where she was busy with the oven.

"One of our cups," said Verity.

"That's all right. She's going to take a little time to learn. She is only very small, after all," said Martha. "Give her a few years and she'll be able to wash all the dishes in this kitchen."

Betty turned her head and stared at the huge cabinets behind her, filled with stacks upon stacks of fine china and silverware, pots and pans, dishes and bowls. Her heart faltered in her chest. How was it that she couldn't drink from those pretty teacups, but someday she had to wash them? What would Verity say if she dropped one of *those*?

And how long would it take to wash *all* the dishes in the kitchen?

Her hands already hurt from scrubbing these few plates and cups. Tears rolled down her cheeks, and she bowed her head over the sink and sobbed.

"Mrs. Evans," yelled Verity, "she's crying again."

Martha bustled into the scullery then, smelling of coal, and grabbed Betty's arm. Her touch was gentle, but it still gave her a fright that made her cry out. The cook crouched down in front of her, her friendly, red-cheeked, doughy face pressed into a strained smile.

"Betty, darling," she said, "this is a kitchen. We don't have time to cry every five minutes. We have to get things done here."

Her tone was soft, and Betty swallowed her tears.

"I need you to concentrate and to do as you're told," said Martha. "Do you understand that? We can't keep the kitchen running if you don't do that. Please, darling."

Betty didn't understand anything except for the tenderness in Martha's eyes. It reminded her of Mama, and like Mama, she felt she would do anything for Martha. Anything. She dragged her knuckles over her eyes and nodded.

"That's my good Little One," said Martha. She kissed Betty's forehead and gave her a cuddle. "That's my *good*, good girl."

Martha went back out to the oven, and Betty turned to the sink, summoning her courage.

"I'm a good girl," she whispered, and pressed her hands into the water.

~ ~ ~ ~ ~

Betty didn't know it was possible to be this tired. Despite the many short naps she'd taken rolled up in a blanket on the hearth rug in the kitchen, her eyelids felt as though they were being held down with leaden weights. Her ankles had been aching fiercely for what felt like forever, and still the kitchen was a hub of feverish chaos.

"Pudding's ready!" Martha barked. "Take it up now. Hurry, hurry!"

Two footmen, harassed and sweating, grabbed trays full of dishes: shortbread and Christmas cake and fruit compotes and meringues, all neatly arrayed on beautiful china dishes and silver trays. They hurried upstairs, and Betty's mouth watered as they passed her by with the delicious-smelling food. She hadn't had anything to eat since lunch, which felt like a hundred years ago. She wondered if they would *ever* have dinner.

"Here," Martha barked, shoving a handful of forks into Betty's small hands. "Wash these, darling, then Verity can do the china."

Betty stumbled to the scullery, mounted her stool for what felt like the ten thousandth time that day, and wearily began to work the hateful sponge over the forks. Their tines were surprisingly sharp and poked her hands painfully as she worked. Her fingers ached constantly, and there were little raw spots on her knuckles, her skin bone dry from the soap and water.

Surely, once she'd finished these forks, that would be the end of it. She would be allowed to have supper and finally go to bed. She could only hope that Martha wouldn't wake her at five in the morning again.

It took the last of her strength to finish the final fork, rinse it, and set it aside for polishing later. She stumbled down from her stool and into the kitchen, where Martha was at work mixing the dough for tomorrow morning's bread.

"I'm all done," she whispered.

"What a good girl." Martha patted the top of her head. "You've been marvellous today." She smiled, and Betty's heart felt instantly lighter. "Now I want you to run along to bed. I can tell you're terribly tired, and I'll bring supper up once we've finished everything."

Betty couldn't decide if she was more hungry or more tired; she decided she was happy to sleep a little before Martha brought her supper. "Thank you."

"Such a good little girl." Martha kissed the top of her head. "Run along, now."

Betty wasn't sure she'd find the way to the servants' quarters, but before she could ask, Martha had turned around and busied herself once again with the dough.

She knew which door they'd come in through, at least. She let herself out of it and climbed a flight of wooden stairs to a landing that separated into two hallways. One led to another stairwell, dark and narrow, going up; the other was broad and pleasant, with a beautifully patterned rug and paintings hanging on the wood-panelled walls. Betty dithered, not sure which way to go, and decided that the narrow stairs looked much too frightening to climb on her own. She hoped that her and Martha's room would be at the end of the broad hallway, so she took it.

Her small, bare feet dug into the lovely rug. It was warm here, and the paintings were so lovely. They showed ladies in beautiful dresses sitting in front of summery windows, stroking little dogs or cats that sat on their laps. There were gentlemen on horses and plump little children on plump little ponies, the children with rosy round cheeks, the ponies with shiny round bottoms.

Voices came from a big door to Betty's left. There was a burst of happy laughter and a snatch of music, and the sound made her slow down. The door was open just a crack, enough that when Betty pressed herself against the doorframe, she could peer into the room.

It was a beautiful drawing-room with a harpsichord, where a pretty woman sat, her fingers dancing over the keys as she teased out the cheerful tune of "Deck the Halls". A group of people stood around her, joining in the song: a boy with round cheeks, a nice-looking old lady with very bright eyes, and a gentleman whose hooked nose made him look miserable even as he mouthed the words of the song. In the corner stood an utterly splendid Christmas tree, sprouting from a room that burst with mistletoe and holly and bunting and tinsel. The tree towered to the ceiling, topped by a pretty white angel just like the one at home.

Betty sang along very quietly, looking at the brown paper parcels piled high beneath the tree. She wondered suddenly if there would be any presents at all for her this Christmas. Maybe one of those pretty parcels was just for her. Miss Parker, for all her snappishness, has taught Betty to read the shape of her own name; if she looked on the labels, she was sure she would find one that said "Betty", B-E-T-T-Y.

She pressed a hand to the door to open it, and a soft voice spoke from behind her. "Oh, hello there!"

Betty spun around. A little boy, perhaps a couple of years older than she was, stood in the hallway. He had softly wavy brown hair, neatly combed, and eyes the deepest shade of emerald-green. They were so dark that it would have been difficult to see their colour if it hadn't been for the warm firelight spilling from the drawing-room, which made them very bright.

"Hello," said Betty.

"You must be Martha's little girl," said the boy. "Grandmama was telling us all about you, even though Father didn't like it."

"Who's Grandmama?" Betty asked.

"She lives in the house," said the boy. He pointed at the nice old lady. "I think Martha calls her Mrs. Bromley."

"Oh," said Betty. Clearly, Mrs. Bromley was the lady who was allowed to drink from the china cups.

"What's your name?" said the boy. "I'm Will. Will Bromley. That's my mama over there by the harpsichord."

"Betty," Betty whispered. She wished she knew her other name, but she didn't. It made Will sound awfully grand that he knew both of his names.

Will smiled, his eyes even brighter. "That's a lovely name. What are you doing out here?"

"I'm looking for my room," said Betty. "I don't know where it is yet." She looked into the drawing-room. "I'm looking for my Christmas present, too."

Will tilted his head to one side. "You didn't get one?"

"No," said Betty.

"That's a shame. Maybe there's one in there for you." Will fumbled in his pocket. "Do you want to see mine? It was in my Christmas cracker."

Betty's eyes widened. "Oh, yes please!"

Will lifted out a small, gleaming, colourful object. A top, Betty realized; one of the little boys at the park she visited with Miss Parker had one. But this one was even prettier than the one she'd seen before. It was brightly polished and painted in stripes of yellow, red and blue.

"Look!" Will crouched down. "I'm no good at whipping it yet, but I can make it spin a little." He put the pointy end down on the floor and gave it a twirl with his wrist. The top swirled, its colours blurring into a rainbow for a moment before it fell over.

"It's so pretty," said Betty. "I love it."

Will picked it up. "Isn't it?" He tilted his head to one side. "When did you come here, anyway? I haven't seen you here before."

"I came to stay here yesterday," said Betty. "Martha found me."

"Martha is lovely." Will paused. "Do you have any toys?"

Betty shrugged. "Not here."

Will looked at the top, then at her. "Here." He held it out.

Betty shrank back. "It's yours."

"No, it's not." Will took her hand and folded it around the top. "It's yours now."

Betty met his eyes. They really were the darkest green imaginable, with thick dark lashes. Pretty eyes, she thought, for a boy.

"Thank you," she said.

"Will!" a hard voice barked from the drawing-room. Betty realized sharply that the music had stopped. "What are you doing out there?"

"I'll see you later." Will said. "You'd better go before Father sees you. He's a grumpy sort."

"Later?" said Betty hopefully.

Will chuckled. "I'll come and find you."

He disappeared into the drawing room, and after a moment's hesitation, Betty shuffled down the hallway with the top clutched firmly in her arms. She held it up to the light as she made her way back toward the kitchen to ask Martha how to get to their room. It sparkled colourfully even when she reached the dark hallway, making the entire room seem filled with light.

This certainly was a very strange Christmas.

Chapter Three

Seven Years Later

Betty hummed to herself as she sliced the carrots, her knife working skilfully over the cutting board, scoring new lines in the wood. Around her, the kitchen was all a-bustle with preparations. The smell of roast beef filled the air, mingling with the ever-present fragrance of the strings of herbs and onions and wood smoke and soap and garlic. Something bubbled on the stove; the fire crackled merrily, and the soft persistent patter of snow on the roof matched the fat white flakes that tumbled in white curtain outside the window, turning the day grey and quiet.

O Christmas tree, O Christmas tree, how lovely are thy branches. The words played through Betty's mind, and she hummed along as she cut the last slice, tossed the carrot top into the bucket for the pigs, and moved the slices into a tureen. She picked up the tureen and turned to the stove, where Martha was feverishly stirring a huge pot.

"Here we are, Martha." Betty set the pot down by Martha's elbow. "The carrots are ready."

"There's a darling. Thank you," said Martha. "How about the potatoes?"

"All peeled and ready to go in the oven whenever we're ready," said Betty.

Martha smiled. "What a clever pet. Look at you Little One! Twelve years old and the most capable little kitchen maid you ever saw."

"You taught me well," said Betty.

Martha patted her cheek. "Precious thing. Have you had tea and a rusk yet?"

"None," said Betty.

"Why, Betty, it's nearly eleven! You must be starving," Martha exclaimed.

Betty laughed. "You haven't had anything either. Nobody has."

"Heavens, child, we'd better do something about that or poor little Annie will faint in the scullery," said Martha. "Make us each a cup while you're waiting to cut the toast for elevenses, that's a good girl."

"Yes, Martha." Betty put the teapot on the stove.

"Sit down a minute, too. You must be tired," said Martha. "It's a dreadful time of year to be in a kitchen, this, with Christmas being only a week away."

"Oh, I'm quite all right," said Betty. "I like Christmas, really."

"It's a hard time at work, but I like Christmas, too." Martha smiled. "How could I not? Christmas is the time when God gave me you."

Betty met her eyes and smiled.

A shrewd look came into Martha's eye. "Then again, I think you and I have different reasons for liking Christmas, don't we?"

"What do you mean?" asked Betty.

Martha gave a throaty chuckle. "Don't pretend you don't know, darling. I've seen you twitching at the curtains every ten minutes, looking to see if a certain carriage has come down the road yet."

Betty felt two spots grow warm in her cheeks.

"I know you've played with Will every Christmas since you were my Little One, darling." Martha's smile faded. "But I have to tell you that you're getting too big for that."

Betty blinked. "I—I beg your pardon?"

"Mr. Bromley won't like it if he sees you," said Martha.

Betty looked away. "We don't let Mr. Bromley see, Martha."

"I know, dear, but he will," said Martha. "I never stopped you before, because when you were little, even Mr. Bromley may have overlooked it. But Will is growing up into a fine young man now, and you into a fine young woman. It's time you each kept to your own circles, and knew your place."

"I don't understand," said Betty.

Martha sighed. "You will, my Little One, in days to come. But for now, you just have to trust me. Stay away from Will Bromley."

The kitchen seemed suddenly much colder. Betty shivered, surprised by the look in Martha's eyes.

Then Martha's features relaxed into a smile. "Besides, we don't have time for play now. We're hosting the Christmas party this weekend! Everything has to be perfect."

The teapot clattered, boiling, and Betty turned to take it off the stove. Before she had time to think about what Martha had said, Verity clattered down the stairs into the kitchen.

"Mrs. Bromley would like jam with her elevenses," she announced.

"Quick, Little One," said Martha. "Get the jam from the pantry."

Betty hurried away.

~ ~ ~ ~ ~

The wind was frigid, and yesterday's snow lay shimmering several inches deep, transforming the green lawns of Bromley House into carpets of white, disturbed only by the tiny tracks of some small animal that had crossed the lawn in the night. Every tree was dusted with snow, as though God Himself had decorated them for Christmas. Every now and then, a tiny break in the clouds would allow a shaft of pure sunlight through, and making the whole world sparkle.

Those glimpses of sunlight were few and far between, and Betty's fingers felt as though they might fall off. She tucked them under her armpits, shivering.

"Why do we all have to stand out here like this?" Annie complained. The little scullery-maid was only ten, and her nose was bright red with cold.

"Mr. Bromley likes it," said Mrs. Coswick, the housekeeper.

The house's full staff stood in a neat row outside the doors, dressed in their best, their collars starched, aprons spotless, shoes polished to a fine shine, ears and noses scarlet with cold as their breath steamed in front of them. Privately, Betty wondered why Mrs. Bromley allowed her son to demand that the servants stood on parade like this, but she supposed that Mrs. Bromley hardly did anything cruel to them compared with the things she'd heard from the maids of other houses. Perhaps one small cruelty a year could be tolerated.

"Look," said Martha, standing beside Betty. "There they come. Look sharp, everybody!"

The servants sprang to attention. With a merry jingle of harness bells and the clop of iron-rimmed hooves, a splendid pair of pure white horses, plumes dancing from their bridles, came up the drive toward them. The brougham they pulled was brightly polished and bore the Bromley family crest on the doors. It rattled to a halt on the drive, and a handsome butler in an elegant tailcoat opened the front door of Bromley House, through which Betty had never walked in her seven years of living here.

It was Adelaide Bromley who now stepped out of the doors. She wore a beautiful silver dress and a coat trimmed with mink, her hat made of matching white fur. A huge, undignified smile was plastered over her features as she descended the steps.

A footman opened the door gracefully, and Harold Bromley stepped out. Betty looked straight past Harold, searching for his son instead. While Harold tried to kiss Adelaide's hand and Adelaide grabbed him in a tight hug instead, Will finally emerged into the sunlight.

He'd grown so much. Betty was startled by how much broader his shoulders were now, and the slightest dusting of hair on his lower jaw. His hair was longer than the last time she'd seen him, and curled even more profusely on his shoulders, softly lustrous.

His eyes were still the deepest green—the green of pine, of an undecorated Christmas tree—and they found hers instantly. A spark came into his eye then, and his lip twitched upward for a moment before he turned his attention to his grandmother.

Betty had to swallow hard to keep herself from crying out. It was never really Christmas to her until she laid eyes on Will, and now her heart raced, thinking of all the time they would be able to spend together over the next few weeks. Suddenly she was no longer cold.

"Oh, Will, my sweetheart!" Adelaide opened her arms wide. "Come to me!"

She wrapped Will in a warm embrace and kissed his cheek, accidentally smearing it with powder. Will chuckled and hugged her tightly. "It's so good to see you, Grandmama."

"My, how you've grown, darling." Adelaide beamed at him. "When did you get so tall?"

"You've only gotten younger," said Will.

Adelaide laughed. "Oh, listen to him!" She waved a hand, then winced; Betty heard an audible creak from her joints. Adelaide smoothed down her sleeves as if to hide her wrists, which had grown so thin that they looked more like fingers, the skin stretched tight over protruding bone. Will's lips flattened into a worried line, but Harold had a different look in his eyes. Something colder, and hungry.

The butler led the family to the house, and Mrs. Coswick exhaled. "All that and he barely even looked at us," she muttered. "Woe betide us the day that this house belongs to him. Come now, everyone. Back inside and back to work. They'll want refreshments at once!"

The staff hurried around the back of the house toward the servants' door at the back of the kitchen. Betty wandered along near the back, smiling, wondering when Will would be able to slip away so that he could see her.

A warm hand closed suddenly on her arm, making her jump.

"Remember what I told you, darling," Martha whispered. "Stay away from Will. No good will come of it."

Betty nodded, unable to agree out loud. Because this was the one time that she wouldn't listen to Martha.

~ ~ ~ ~ ~

Betty ran the damp cloth over the kitchen table and glanced around the room with a small sigh of relief. It was lunchtime, and the servants had all eaten; then Betty and Annie had been left to clear the plates and wash the dishes, only to clean up the kitchen and start all over again with preparations for the family's tea. Now, at least, Betty could snatch a few minutes to sit down and have a cup of tea before the chaos began anew.

She put the teapot on the stove. "Martha, would you like some?"

Martha was checking the pastry she had in the oven. She closed it and wiped her hands on her apron. "No thank you, dear. My feet are killing me today—I think I'll go have a little lie down for a few minutes."

"That's a good idea," said Betty. "I'll have a cup of tea and then get started on cutting the vegetables you put on the list for me." She nodded toward the handwritten list that Martha had scribbled for her. Martha had taught her how to read and write a few words; it wasn't much, but it was enough to know how many potatoes, turnips and beets she had to prepare for tea.

"Thank you, Little One." Martha patted the top of her head. "I'm lucky to have you."

She climbed the stairs out of the kitchen a little more stiffly than she used to, and Betty watched her with worry building in her belly. She dismissed it quickly. Adelaide loved Martha; she would be sure to care for her even when she grew older.

Woe betide us the day this house belongs to him. Mrs. Coswick's words echoed unexpectedly in Betty's mind, and her body grew stiff with fear.

The soft tap at the window made her jump, almost spilling hot tea on herself. She peered through it, seeing nothing at first. Then, a pebble bounced off the glass, reproducing the sound. It was soft enough that one would barely pay attention to it in a bustling kitchen full of people. Now, it made Betty smile.

She scrambled to make two cups of tea—tin cups, of course—and carried them out of the back door and down the garden path to the great old Scots pine that grew at the corner of the vegetable patch. It was a massive tree, so ancient that its trunk was as gnarled and wrinkled as Adelaide's face, and its branches were so tightly matted and swept so low that the ground beneath it was free of snow. Betty had always thought of it as the giant Christmas tree.

Betty squeezed through a gap in the branches—it had been easier to fit through last year—and felt the cold kiss of snow as it brushed onto her clothes. Will sat comfortably on one of the tree's twisted roots, perfect as a Christmas gift.

"Betty!" He jumped to his feet. "Oh, look! You've brought tea."

"I'm the kitchen maid now," said Betty proudly. "I make tea for everybody." She held out a cup.

"I've never drunk from a tin cup before," said Will with a laugh. He took the cup from her and sipped. "Ooh, you make very good tea."

Betty felt warmth flood to her cheeks. "Thank you!"

She perched on a root opposite him and sipped the hot liquid, grateful for its warmth; the branches did not completely block the freezing wind.

"How has school been?" she asked.

Will pulled a face. "My second year there has been no better than the first."

"You *sound* like someone who goes to school," Betty teased.

Will groaned. "I know! Isn't it appalling?"

"Appalling?" Betty giggled. "What does that mean?"

"It means that I'm turning into a real prig," said Will.

Betty laughed. "I don't think so."

"Well, good." Will grinned. "I don't want to be a stuck-up prig like my father. I'd much rather be like Grandmama—a little bit of a rogue."

"Mrs. Bromley is lovely. We're so lucky to work for her," said Betty. "She never beats me, and she makes sure we're paid a good living wage, Martha says. I'm almost old enough to earn one."

"Of course. Grandmama often talks about how much of a shame it is that so many of us treat our servants badly," said Will. "It always makes Father very embarrassed." He grimaced. "I'm sorry you all had to stand out in the cold like that when we got here yesterday."

"It's all right," said Betty. "I got to see you all the sooner."

The words spilled out before she could stop them, and Will suddenly went very quiet. It felt as though his eyes were looking right into her heart. She wondered what they saw there, if he had a name for the feeling that tingled all the way down to her toes, if he knew that her heart was now thudding so hard against her ribs that she thought it might break free.

His face relaxed into a smile. "Well, I was happy to see you, too Little One." He sipped the last of his tea. "Hey, I brought a new game. I think it might be a boys' game, but I don't see why you can't play." He pulled a small pouch from his pocket. "Have you ever played marbles before?"

"No," said Betty.

"That's all right." Will crouched down and cleared the leaf litter away from a circle of dirt. "I'll show you."

Betty scooted nearer, arms wrapped around herself against the cold. But despite the wind, here with Will, she'd never felt warmer.

35

Chapter Four

Betty pressed her back against the wall as Verity hurried down the kitchen stairs. Ever since she'd become a parlour-maid, Verity walked everywhere with her nose held high, and this was no exception. She stalked past Betty to the scullery and planted a tray full of dirty dishes beside the sink.

"Make sure not to chip anything," she said snidely to Annie.

The little scullery-maid blinked back tears. "I won't."

"You did this morning," said Verity. "You're lucky I saw the chip in the teacup, since even Betty didn't." She gave Betty a sneer.

Annie's eyes filled with tears. "It wasn't there when I put it in the cupboard!"

"I must have bumped it when I was making tea," said Betty soothingly. "Verity, I think the cheeseboard and wine is ready to go up."

Verity curled her lip at Betty, then strode over to the cheeseboard waiting on the kitchen table. Betty shook her head and turned her attention back to cleaning out the oven.

One of the footmen appeared at the top of the stairs. "Mrs. Evans!" he called. "They've changed their mind. They don't want wine tonight; they'd like port instead."

"Port with cheese?" Martha chuckled. "That'll give Harold the collywobbles, but I know that's how Adelaide likes it. All right, Victor, go and fetch the wine glasses down or they'll be in the way. We'll have to send the port glasses up instead."

"I can't carry all that by myself," said Verity.

"Well, we can't let the guests wait, can we?" said Martha sharply. "Betty, go up with Verity and help her. Just make sure that you're not seen, all right?"

"Of course." Betty got up from her knees, washed her hands hastily and donned a clean bonnet. She stacked port glasses neatly on a silver tray while Verity fetched the bottle from the cellar, and then they both clattered up the stairs.

As a kitchen maid, Betty seldom ventured beyond her downstairs world. A trip up to the main house always felt like an adventure. She focused on keeping her tray steady as she followed Verity down the elegant hallway where she'd first met Will. The memory made her smile. Music poured from the ballroom just down the hall tonight, too, but this was a merry dance played on the violin, and the elegant patter of dancing feet accompanied it.

The footman was on his way out with the wine glasses when they arrived. "Hurry," he hissed. "Mr. Bromley isn't happy about the change."

"Mr. Bromley is never happy," said Betty contentedly. "Here, Victor, take these port glasses and I'll go downstairs with the wine glasses."

"Thanks, Betty."

Verity pushed past them into the ballroom, and Betty and Victor nervously exchanged trays with barely a cling of crystal.

Victor bustled into the ballroom with the port glasses, and Betty retreated behind the doorway. She couldn't resist peering into this other world—the world inhabited by those who were allowed to drink from china teacups—as she stood outside, holding the tray of wine glasses.

The ballroom looked splendid. Mistletoe and bunting were draped all over the room, dangling in sweeping arcs from the ceiling. There was a Christmas tree in the corner of this room, too, wrapped in tasteful yellow ribbon, with glass baubles dangling from every service and china reindeer chasing one another in circles from top to bottom.

Elegant guests, men in their beautifully cut suits and women with fur-trimmed dresses, stood by the crackling fire and talked in soft, low voices. Only a handful of people danced, but they did so with smiling faces. Gifts were piled high on the table by the Christmas tree, wrapped in brown paper with gaudy ribbons.

Betty smiled. This wasn't her world, but it was lovely to look at.

Verity and Victor set down their trays on the long table on one side of the room. Betty watched as Harold detached himself from his timid little wife and strode over to them, looking thunderous. Adelaide, sitting near the table in her favourite armchair, grabbed his arm before he could reach them. She shook her head sharply, and Harold relented.

Betty took a step back. She had better return to the kitchen before she was missed, but suddenly she wondered if Will would be at the party.

He must be old enough to attend these now. She leaned forward, searching the crowd of dancers, and the sudden clash of breaking glass tore through the ballroom.

The violin faltered, a wrong note rising in a squeak from the instrument.

The player recovered himself quickly, but every guest in the room was still looking around for the source of the sound. Betty spotted it instantly. Verity stood by the table, hands clasped to her mouth, glass lying shattered on the ground at her feet.

Betty's belly twisted into knots. Verity had dropped a crystal port glass.

"You!" Harold snapped, his voice low and cold.

"Harold!" Adelaide half rose from her chair, then turned white and sagged back into it.

Harold seized Verity by the arm. Betty retreated and ducked behind an elderly but often-polished suit of armour a little way down the hall. A moment later, Harold dragged Verity into the hallway. The girl was crying, clutching her empty tray.

"I'm sorry, sir. It slipped out of my hand," she sobbed. "It just slipped out—"

Harold drew back a hand to strike her. Verity cried out and cringed, and Harold froze.

"You can be grateful that my mother is a pathetic, pitying woman," he hissed, "or I would mark your face right now for your clumsiness." He shook Verity hard and let her go, and she reeled down the hallway, clutching the tray with both hands. "See that this never happens again. You have ashamed me before all the high society of London."

"Yes, sir. Yes, sir," Verity whimpered. "I'm sorry, sir."

"Get out of my sight," Harold snarled.

Verity scampered down the hallway. Harold smoothed a hand over his hair, straightened the front of his jacket, and returned to the ballroom, shutting the door quietly behind him.

Betty swallowed hard. Again, she heard Mrs. Coswick's voice in her mind. *Woe betide...*

She pushed the thought away and scampered down the hall after Verity. It would be a long time yet, she hoped. A very long time yet before Harold was the master of this house.

~ ~ ~ ~ ~

When Betty clattered into the kitchen, Martha stood open-mouthed by the stove, halfway through pouring eggnog.

"Betty!" she cried. "What happened? Verity just threw down her tray and ran weeping through the kitchen. I think she's gone up to her room."

"Mr. Bromley shouted at her and shook her, Martha," said Betty. "It was awful!"

"But why?" asked Martha.

"She dropped one of the port glasses, but it was only an accident," said Betty. "Mrs. Bromley wasn't angry at all. She tried to stop him."

"He's had a mean temper on him, that Harold, ever since he was a youngster," Martha muttered darkly. "He had just left school when I first started working here and I was only too grateful when he married poor little Amelia and went to live in the house that he'd inherited on their marriage. I would have hated to work under him."

"He was very cruel," said Betty.

"I suppose that's why Adelaide was only too happy to see him go." Martha sighed. "All right. Did someone clean up the glass?"

"No," said Betty, "and there's still another cheeseboard to take up. Victor is pouring the port; the guests were getting restless."

"There's nothing else for it, then." Marta opened a cupboard and pulled out a freshly starched uniform. "Get changed, Betty. You'll have to serve the guests."

"But I'm only a kitchen maid," Betty cried.

"Tonight, you're a parlour-maid—at least until I can get Verity to stop blubbering and go back in there." Marta held out the uniform. "All you need to do is to carry the cheeseboard up and sweep away the glass. Hide your brush and scoop in your apron pocket. There's a good girl."

Betty scrambled into the clean uniform in the lavatory, then hurried to wash her hands and take up the cheeseboard, her apron bulging with what she needed to clean up the glass. Her heart was beating very quickly as she hesitated at the ballroom door. All her life, she had been told to stay away, to avoid being seen, but now she had to step out in front of all the guests.

She took a deep breath and walked into the ballroom.

Immediately, she felt Harold glaring at her. He stood at the back of the room, his wife hanging on his arm, talking with some other self-important men. His eyes followed her all the way across the room, but Betty kept her back very straight and carried the cheeseboard with grace, and when she set it on the white tablecloth, Harold had looked away.

"Thank heaven you're here," Victor hissed. "I've been standing on the glass all this time to keep the guests away. Where's Verity?"

"Mrs Evans has her busy downstairs Sir," Betty whispered. "Can you shield me from the guests?"

Victor nodded and stepped forward. Betty ducked behind his legs, his coattails hanging down to his knees, and hastily fished her brush and scoop out of her pocket.

As she worked the bits of glass out of the thick carpet, Betty risked a quick scan of the ballroom again, still looking for Will.

She spotted dark curls bouncing on the dance floor—and it was him. For a moment, she could only stare. Will was wearing a tailcoat himself, and he looked wonderfully grown up with his cream waistcoat and matching tie. Her breath caught in her chest, and she nearly dropped the brush.

Then she saw her. A girl, wrapped elegantly in Will's arms. She was the prettiest in the room, Betty could tell at a single glance. She looked as though she had stepped right from the pages of *Snow White*, with her pitch-dark hair, red lips and pale skin, her eyes as blue as the summer sky.

Will stared over the top of the girl's head as he twirled her around the dance floor. He was so graceful, and she moved in perfect time with him, her lovely blue dress stirring only slightly as she danced. She looked like she was floating.

She looked perfect.

"Betty?" Victor hissed. "There's guests coming!"

Betty scrambled to sweep up the last of the glass. She tipped the scoop and brush into her apron pocket and straightened, smoothing her dress over her knees. Now she only had to make her escape. But a gaggle of guests headed toward the table, obscuring her path. Betty moved to one side and stood patiently at the end of the table, hands laced behind her back, just like she'd seen Verity do. She glanced at Harold, but he wasn't looking her way. Adelaide, though, caught her eye, and the old lady gave her a broad smile.

Betty exhaled a tiny breath of relief. She was doing all right.

"Just look at those two!" said one of the ladies leaning against the wall near Betty. "Have you ever seen such a handsome young couple?"

"Young couple? They're only fourteen years old," said another. "I'd hardly call them a couple."

"Who?" said a third. "Will Bromley and Olive Hilton?"

"Yes, those two." The first woman laughed. "Aren't they wonderful to look at?"

Betty's stomach tied itself in a knot. She swallowed hard, her cheeks flushing, sweat breaking out on her palms.

"They *are* very good together," said the second, "but how can you call them a couple?"

"You know that Harold Bromley and Gareth Hilton have been friends since they were at school together," said the first. "When Will and Olive were born in the same year, well, it was written in the stars, wasn't it?"

"I wonder if they agree," said the third.

Betty didn't understand. Could they be saying what she feared they were saying?

"I don't think they have a choice," said the first. "They were practically engaged at birth, if their parents have anything to do with it."

All three ladies tittered sickeningly, and Betty could no longer bear it. Her route to the door was clear. She hurried across the carpet as quickly as she could, but she was not yet halfway when she heard a soft voice calling her name.

"Betty! Betty, dear."

It was Adelaide. Even though Betty's heart pounded furiously and she longed to escape this room and run into Martha's arms, she stopped and turned around, curtseying neatly to her mistress. "Yes, ma'am?"

Adelaide held out a hand. "Come here."

Betty hastened to the old lady's side. Adelaide's face was suddenly very pale, and when she breathed, Betty heard an alarming crackle in her chest.

"Are you well, ma'am?" Betty asked nervously.

"Yes, yes, I'm fine, dear," said Adelaide, but there were beads of sweat on her upper lip. "Could you—would you get me a glass of water, please? Only water. Thank you."

"Of course, ma'am." Betty curtseyed again. "Are—are you sure you're all right?"

"Don't fuss Betty." Adelaide waved a hand. "Just get my water, please."

"Yes, ma'am." Betty hastened to the water jug on the end of the table and poured a tumbler of water for Adelaide, then placed it on a small tray. She returned to the old lady's side and proffered the tray gracefully, as she'd seen Verity do.

"You do a fine job as a—" Adelaide winced, coughed painfully, then smiled again. "A fine job as a parlour-maid, dear."

"Thank you, ma'am," said Betty.

Adelaide took the glass and managed a small sip. Betty glanced over her shoulder at the dance floor; the tune had changed, but Will still danced with the beautiful Olive Hilton, and something frightened and ugly curled in the pit of Betty's stomach.

Practically engaged at birth.

The thought made her toes curl.

She forced her attention back to Adelaide. The old lady was hunched forward now, her breaths coming in painful wheezes, and the glass trembled dangerously in her hand.

Betty grabbed it before it could fall. "Ma'am?" she said. "Ma'am?"

Adelaide's face turned ashen. She pitched forward, and before Betty could move, she crumpled to the floor.

"Ma'am!" Betty cried. She fell to her knees, placing the tray on the ground. "Mrs. Bromley!"

"Mother!" Harold almost sent Betty sprawling as he rushed to Adelaide's side. "Dr. Joseph? Dr. Joseph!"

A well-dressed man with a monocle shouldered his way through the crowd. Betty grabbed the tray before he could step on it, and he shoved her out of the way. She juggled the tray, trying not to drop the glass, and when it stopped wobbling the crowd around Adelaide was so thick that Betty could no longer see her.

She didn't know what to do. All she saw was Harold, glaring all around him, looking for someone to blame. The anger in his face made her heart stop.

Woe betide us the day...

Betty turned and fled from the ballroom, tears gathering in her eyes. Adelaide had to be all right. She had to get better, or they would all lose the mistress they loved—and the kindness she'd always shown them.

Chapter Five

Martha's eyes were bloodshot from lack of sleep. She blinked them painfully as she carved the last slice from the pork roast, letting it fall neatly onto the ornate dish.

"Hurry up, Betty!" she barked. "Get this upstairs!"

Betty looked up, dismayed. "I'm still busy making the roux for the pudding, Martha."

"Let me do that," Martha snapped, grabbing the spoon from her and working it furiously over the pan. "Hurry!"

Betty blinked away tears at Martha's harsh tone. She grabbed the gravy boat as Victor seized the huge dish of pork, and they scrambled up the stairs together.

"Still no sign of Verity?" Victor whispered.

"None," said Betty. "I wish she'd come back. I can't keep doing the work of a kitchen-maid and a parlour maid."

Victor grimaced. "Where do you think she went?"

Betty shrugged. "Maybe she left. She was like that."

Victor's face grew sombre. "Verity could be sharp, but she wouldn't be foolish enough to leave in the dead of winter. Where do you suppose she would ever go?"

Betty thought of Martha's snappishness and the way she refused to talk about Verity, even to hear her name. "You don't think she's been dismissed, do you? Mrs. Bromley would never do such a thing over a broken glass."

"I don't think Mrs. Bromley made the decision," said Victor quietly.

They both fell into a respectful silence as they passed the staircase that led up to the bedrooms. Earlier, they had set only four places at the table instead of five.

"Tomorrow is Christmas Eve," Betty murmured. "Surely she'll be back at the table by then."

"I hope so," said Victor, "for all of our sakes."

~ ~ ~ ~ ~

It was past midnight. Betty's arms ached with exhaustion as she kneaded the dough for the following morning's bread, punching it down, folding it over, pressing it together, flipping it and starting again. The dough went from sticky to smooth in her hands, but this time, she took no pleasure in watching the process. All she wanted was to be done with it so that she could finally go to bed.

Her hands trembled with weakness as she set the dough on the windowsill to rise and rubbed her burning eyes, thinking of everything she had to do. She had to air out the parlour before breakfast tomorrow morning, by which time she would have had to sweep the floors, gather the eggs, put the bread in the oven... The list droned on in her mind, and Betty longed for sleep.

She was about to take off her apron when the bell jangled for Adelaide's room. Weariness swamped her body. Ordinarily, her lady's maid would answer the bell, but she hadn't left

Adelaide's side since her collapse at the Christmas party. Betty would have to go and see what she needed, then make the long trek back down to the kitchen for whatever was required.

Don't sigh so, Little One. Be grateful for what we have. Martha had said those words a thousand times to her that day, and they made her nervous. She'd sent Martha up to bed earlier; her hands were sore and twisted with rheumatism, and Betty feared she wouldn't be able to work at all tomorrow if she didn't rest. She was alone in the kitchen, so she traipsed up the stairs all on her own.

Ella, the lady's maid, stood timorously outside Adelaide's door when Betty plodded down the hallway. Her eyes were still red from her own bout with influenza; she had been sick in bed the night of the Christmas party. It was as though she blamed herself for the fact that Adelaide had collapsed. Her face was pinched with exhaustion.

"Oh, Betty, there you are," she whispered. "I know this is an unusual hour, but Mrs. Bromley is awake for the first time all day and she says she thinks she could drink a little soup. Do you still have any in the kitchen?"

Betty's heart failed within her. She stared at Ella for a few long moments, thinking of the walk back down to the kitchen, of stoking the stove and placing the pot of leftover soup on it, waiting for it to bubble, taking out the necessary dish, tray and spoon, dishing it up and then climbing all of these stairs to this top room. It was a small task, perhaps, but Betty's day had consisted of hundreds of these small tasks, strung and strung and strung together so that she had been on her feet for close to twenty hours now.

She wanted to tell Ella to do it herself, but she read utter exhaustion in the dark circles under Ella's eyes, and at that moment she heard it: a terrible, rattling cough. The sound reminded her sharply that there was a woman behind that door who, for all the pampered privilege in which she had lived her life, now suffered far more than Betty did.

"Yes, of course," she said. "There's plenty of the cream of chicken soup we made for supper."

"Thank you, Betty," said Ella, her shoulders sagging. "I know that if she could only have a bite to eat, perhaps she would rally."

"How is she?" Betty asked.

Ella's eyes filled with tears, and the corners of her mouth drew sharply down. She was no longer a young woman, and Martha had told Betty once that she had spent her entire working life in Adelaide's service.

"She's holding on," Ella whispered, and vanished behind the door.

~ ~ ~ ~ ~

Betty could scarcely believe it.

It was Christmas Eve, and the Bromleys had cancelled the family gathering that usually took place that evening. Only four would dine: Will, his parents and his younger brother. By the time they sent word down to the kitchen, Betty had already peeled enough potatoes for twelve people, but she had not yet started on the other vegetables or the dough.

The reason behind the cancellation saddened her—clearly, her cream of chicken soup had not been enough to cure Adelaide, and she was still ailing too much for the family to want a party—but she couldn't fail to miss the implication: Betty now had far more time than she had expected to have. She wouldn't have to wait on guests, for one thing. Her kitchen work was hugely reduced, for another.

It was a blissful relief to make herself a cup of tea knowing that she would be allowed to sit down to drink it. She cupped it in her hands and went to sit down on the stool by the window, but a stirring caught her eye outside. It was the bough of the pine tree, the undecorated Christmas tree, stirring in the breeze.

Betty smiled at the sight. She knew exactly where she would go for this precious, stolen moment. She glanced at the clock; it was not yet two in the afternoon, which meant that Harold and his wife would still be in their bedroom, taking their afternoon rest. That was the time when Will usually came down to the tree to meet her.

She hurriedly made a second tin cup and carried them both outside. It was a strangely beautiful day, considering that it was Christmas Eve. Bitterly cold, the snow lying knee deep, but beautiful, nonetheless. The snow had stopped for long enough that the gardener had shovelled a comfortable path through the garden, and Betty strolled easily between the white banks, glimmering in the rare winter sun. The sky was absolutely blue above her, bright as a blue diamond.

She was smiling despite her exhaustion as she squeezed between the branches. "I'm so sorry I couldn't come earlier," she called softly. "I was—"

She stopped. The space beneath the tree was empty except for the crisp smell of pine needles and a single red robin, perched on the root where Will usually sat. He chirped once, then flew away with a buzz of tiny wings.

Betty's shoulders sagged. Will must be in the house, perhaps checking on his sick grandmother. Of course he wouldn't have time to come and see her; this must cause almost as much

51

turmoil for him as it did for her. Betty sank down onto the root where he usually sat, clutching the two mugs, and took a long sip from one. At least this was a nice spot to sit, she told herself, trying to counteract the disappointment that spread thickly through her heart.

She was taking her second sip when she heard laughter—the laughter of a young girl. Betty couldn't imagine that any of the servant girls would have reason to laugh like that at a time like this. Then she heard a voice, deep and melodic and familiar.

Will.

A terrible suspicion grew in her like a cancer. She tried to dismiss it, but it metastasized when she squeezed between the branches and peered out in the direction of the sound.

It had come from the stable yard, and now so did the clopping of hooves. Two horses strode from the yard, beautifully groomed, their manes plaited with bits of holly, their hooves oiled and tails trimmed. One was the old pony that Adelaide had kept for Will; the other was the lithe, big-boned hack, his first full-sized horse, that his family had brought along. Will was riding it skilfully despite its size. His pony trotted along beside him, keeping up with a good will, and Olive sat side-saddle on its back.

Betty's fingers clenched tightly on the ears of the mugs until the tin pressed hard into her skin.

Even she could see that Olive couldn't ride. She clutched the front of the saddle and bounced, the reins hanging loosely from the bridle.

"Will!" she squeaked. "I'm going to fall off!"

Will stopped his horse, and the pony obligingly came to a halt beside it. "We don't have to go out for a ride, if you'd rather not."

Olive shook her head fiercely. "No, no. I want to go."

"Well, hold your reins shorter, then," said Will, a frown wrinkling his eyebrows.

Olive fumbled with the reins, and Will tapped his horse with his heels. The horse ambled onward, tossing its head and frisky in the crisp air, but he held it back so that the plodding pony could keep up.

"You're ever such a good rider, Will," Olive trilled, dropping a rein. "Did they teach you at school?"

A shadow crossed Will's face. "No," he said. "Grandmama taught me."

"She'll be all right," said Olive flatly.

Will looked away, silent. Oblivious to the pain in his face, Olive twittered on about his equestrian prowess, and they disappeared down the drive toward the park, leaving Betty alone underneath the damp old pine tree with two cups of tea growing cold in her hands.

~ ~ ~ ~ ~

It hardly felt like Christmas Eve without a pile of dishes to wash. Betty glanced at the clock as she gave the dough a last punch and set it aside to rise; ten minutes to ten, and she was just about finished with her work. She couldn't wait to go upstairs and crawl into her little bunk in Martha's room.

Victor popped his head around the scullery door. "Did you hear?"

Annie jumped, almost dropping a fork.

"Did I hear what?" Betty asked.

Victor lowered his voice. "They sent for the doctor again, right before supper."

Betty frowned. "They did? But he was here this morning."

"I know. Something must be going wrong," said Victor.

"Nonsense," Martha barked sharply. She stood over the stove, rubbing her sore and swollen knuckles, which were bright red tonight. "Don't go around spreading sensation, Victor. It's no use to anyone. Why don't you go and do something useful instead?"

Victor ducked his head and wisely retreated to his corner of the kitchen to polish shoes.

Martha tutted, shaking her head, and picked up the menu she'd written for tomorrow's breakfast. Pinching the paper between thumb and forefinger, she winced.

"Oh, Martha, your poor hands," said Betty. "They look so sore tonight."

"They'll be all right, darling," said Martha. "Mrs. Bromley will be all right, too." She took a steadying breath. "Everything will be all right."

Betty wasn't sure who Martha was trying to convince. She set out the bread to rise and checked that Annie had put away all the silverware. Then, with hands that ached with work, she untied her apron strings, folded the apron and set it in the laundry basket for the housemaid to wash.

"I think we're all done," she said.

"Yes, I suppose so." Martha stretched. "It's time we went up to bed. We'll have plenty to do tomorrow to make sure they have a right Christmas feast for lunch."

"Do you think they'll want a feast, with Mrs. Bromley being so ill?" Betty asked.

"Mrs. Bromley is going to be fine." Martha's voice broke. "She's going to be all right, and everything will be all right. You'll see."

Her words were scarcely cold when there was a dreadful, unearthly sound from upstairs; a long, sobbing wail, brief and breathless, echoing through the stories of the great house.

"What was *that*?" Betty cried.

The colour had bled from Martha's face. Betty had never seen her so deathly pale.

"A cat," she croaked. "It must have been a cat."

"It didn't *sound* like a cat," said Annie.

Martha sat down sharply in a chair. "Must have been a cat," she whispered.

Running feet sounded on the stairs to the kitchen. A moment later, Ella burst into the room, her grey head bent, her face cradled in her hands. She stumbled to a halt by the fire, sobbing incessantly, and her knees buckled.

Victor leaped up from his corner and grabbed Ella's arms. "Quick!" he cried. "She's fainting. Do something!"

Betty ran for a pail of water—she had no idea what she was going to do with it, but it seemed to be the right thing—but Ella didn't faint. She only crumpled into a heap, half supported by Victor, and wept in great, loud, keening sobs that scared Betty to her very core. She had never heard a human being make such terrible sounds.

"Stop that, Ella!" Martha barked. "Pull yourself together and for Pete's sake, tell us what happened!"

Her words only made Ella sob all the harder, and it was several long minutes before she finally raised her face from her hands. She was a pale ghost with a throbbing red nose and tears streaming down her wrinkled cheeks.

"Oh, Adelaide!" she sobbed. "Oh, my mistress, Adelaide!"

"What about her?" Martha asked sharply.

Betty read the answer in Ella's eyes, and her strength drained from her. She stood shaking on the kitchen floor, her breaths coming in ragged gulps, the words running through her mind over and over: *Woe betide us.*

Ella's face crumpled, her mouth a gaping, graceless, drooling pit of sorrow. "She's dead!"

"No!" Annie cried.

"Are you sure?" asked Victor.

"She was holding my hand, and then she was gone. Her eyes went dead. So empty," Ella wailed. "Then the doctor listened to her chest, and he said—he said—" She burst into tears once more.

"No," Martha whispered. She reeled back a few steps and grabbed the nearest chair. "Oh, no. No." Tears filled her eyes, the first that Betty had ever seen there. "Oh, Adelaide, may God rest your gentle soul."

She sagged into the chair, and Betty realized that she was crying too, her tears hot on her cheeks. It seemed unthinkable, impossible even, that the sweet old lady with her gentle voice could be gone. She was the pillar of this house's existence, the solid ground on which Betty stood, and now she had crumbled to dust.

"What's going to happen to us, Martha?" she cried. "What's going to happen?"

Martha pressed her sore hands to her face, and sobs racked her body. It was that sight, the sight of Martha crying, that told Betty that everything was about to change.

Chapter Six

Betty woke the next morning to a storm.

She lay in bed for a few moments in the dark, listening to the wind howling around the house. Handfuls of snow slammed into the shuttered window, and the roof roared under the storm's onslaught. Betty felt as though that same storm now raged inside her.

"Betty, come on," Martha whispered, turning up the lamp and filling their tiny room with golden light.

Betty dragged herself out of bed and into her uniform. Somehow she found the wherewithal to plaster down her hair and tie it up neatly, then to slip on her bonnet and tie the strings under her chin. The movements felt pointless and futile; her fingers seemed stupid, almost incapable of making the simple knot. What good was it now to go down to that kitchen and start cooking? It felt as though the whole world was about to end.

She shuffled to the door, and Martha laid a hand on her arm. "Betty—"

Betty looked up. "Yes?"

Martha attempted a smile despite her red, swollen eyes, which told Betty that she had not slept at all last night. "Merry Christmas," she croaked.

The words felt wispy and hollow, and they blew away on the storm wind so that Betty couldn't manage to say them back. She only tried to smile, then hurried downstairs to the kitchen.

The same old routine felt grey and lifeless. Buttered toast and bacon, salmon and boiled eggs, all made and sent up for breakfast. Betty helped Annie with the dishes and tried to come up with answers for all the questions the little girl had. "Is Mrs. Bromley in Heaven now?" "Do you think she likes it there?" "Will I get influenza and die, too?" The worst one of all: "What will happen to us now?"

"I don't know," said Betty, truthfully.

As soon as the breakfast dishes were done and cleared away, they got started on the goose. Betty had plucked it the day before, when there still seemed to be any hope. She washed it now and set it on a tray for Martha to prepare, and she felt as naked and defenceless as that dead goose.

She was about to get started on peeling the potatoes when Mrs. Coswick strode into the kitchen, her high-collared dress forcing her chin even higher than usual. The older woman folded her hands in front of her and cleared her throat, as if struggling to find her voice; her eyes were red, too.

"Everyone," she said at length.

Betty looked up from her work, and Martha paused in rubbing salt and oil on the goose.

"Mr. Bromley has asked to see us all in the entrance hall," said Mrs. Coswick. "Now, I know that this is difficult, but I expect you will present yourselves at your very best for him."

She turned and stalked away, and Betty looked at Martha. "Why does he want to see us?"

"I don't know, darling." Martha set her jaw. "Come on. We don't want to keep him waiting. Put on a clean apron, there's a dear."

Betty scrambled into a freshly starched apron and followed Martha upstairs to the entrance hall. She had only been here a few times, and that was recently, covering for Verity as a parlour-maid, when she helped female guests with their coats. Mrs. Coswick was already there, standing with her heels neatly together and her hands folded in front of her. Her pale, wrinkled throat trembled as she watched them come into the room.

Right beside her stood Harold Bromley.

His back was as straight as the severely clipped line of his moustache, as the parting in his hair, the same colour as Will's but combed to ferocious neatness. His wife hovered timorously nearby, and the two boys were there, too. Betty's gaze flew immediately to Will, and her heart squeezed at the sight of him. His eyes were damp, and he stared at the carpet with hunched shoulders that trembled slightly as though he was trying not to cry.

Betty's heart went out to him, but she dared not say anything. Instead she followed Martha to the line of servants and took her place between the housemaid and Annie, all in their neat black-and-white uniforms.

"They are all here, sir," said Mrs. Coswick.

Harold nodded to her curtly and marched down the line of servants, from the stately butler at one end to poor little Annie at the other. Betty tried not to tremble as he stalked past them. When he stopped in front of her, her heart quaked in her chest.

"You," he growled. "Who are you?"

"Betty Evans, sir." Betty curtseyed. "The kitchen-maid."

"And a very useless kitchen-maid too," Harold barked. "Look at those uneven bonnet strings!"

Betty froze.

Harold's slap came out of nowhere. His hand ran across the back of Betty's head, a light cuff that barely hurt, but the impact of being struck purposefully by the man towering over her made her cower and cry out.

"Be quiet," Harold barked. "Tie your bonnet strings properly. I will not have such shenanigans in my house."

"Yes, sir. Sorry, sir," Betty squeaked.

"I told you to be *quiet*!" Harold yelled.

Betty cringed before him, fumbling with those strings, and he turned to sweep his cold gaze across the assembled servants. Martha's eyes were as round as full moons.

"You have all been accustomed to a certain expectation of order in this house," he said. "That is to say, no order whatsoever. My mother, God rest her soul, allowed you to become a slovenly and undisciplined rabble. I will not have that happening in my house."

My house? Betty's heart froze.

"You have a new master now." Harold's eyes glittered with imperious delight. "You can expect absolute order from this moment forward. I will have no mess and no disarray in my house. I will have no lack of discipline. I will have perfection. Do I make myself clear?"

Even Mrs. Coswick looked daunted, but she mustered up the courage to say, "Yes, sir."

"Dismissed," Harold snarled. "And see to it that my Christmas luncheon is fit for the new master of a house."

He turned on his heel and stalked away, leaving Betty and the other servants quaking in his wake.

Woe betide us indeed, Betty thought.

~ ~ ~ ~ ~

Betty sat at the kitchen table with her head in her hands, taking slow, deep breaths to hold back the weight of the tears that had gathered in her chest.

It was the most miserable Christmas in all the world.

The pall of Adelaide's passing and Harold's speech that morning hung thickly over the kitchen, a choking cloud of dismay that made it hard to breathe. The love and joy that had once filled the room was gone now. They had basted the goose, cooked the pudding, and cut the Christmas cake in quaking silence, striving to make every morsel perfect. Betty had arranged the gravy boat with shaking hands, desperate not to miss a single drop even as her eyes burned from lack of sleep.

Now, at last, every plate had gone up and every dish had been eaten, and there had been no dire threats from the floors above. Betty still had a full afternoon's work in front of her—the kitchen was dirty and chaotic from all the work—but her relief made her want to weep.

~ ~ ~ ~ ~

The familiar tap of a pebble on glass made her raise her head. No one else in the kitchen looked up; it was a quiet sound, one that the others barely noticed, but a part of Betty had been listening for it all day. Most of the servants were filing through to their dining hall, where Martha had conjured up lunch for them in the midst of the chaos. It would be somewhat festive, Betty knew: roast chicken with vegetables, a mound of soft white rice, rolls and even a black pudding. But Betty's hunger was for something deeper than food at that moment.

61

She slipped out of the door and into the storm, ignoring the biting wind through her clothes. Reaching the tree was a quest in itself, but she fought her way through the wind and snow until she pushed through the branches and into the comparative peace beneath them.

This time, Will was waiting. He sat on a large root, hugging himself, his face pale and streaked with tears. When he saw her, a wan smile found its way to his lips.

"Betty," he croaked.

"Oh, Will," said Betty. "Oh, Will, I'm so sorry about your grandmama."

Will's lower lip trembled, and for a moment she thought he would cry right in front of her. Then he dragged his sleeve over his eyes and struggled manfully for control of his voice. "I'll miss her always, Betty. There'll never be a moment that I won't be missing her."

"Me too," said Betty, the tears spilling over. "I don't know what we're going to do without her." She sagged onto her usual seat on the root opposite him.

Will reached out helplessly and patted her shoulder, a small and awkward movement, but she saw the heart behind it and was grateful for it.

"I'm sorry about the way Papa talked to you Little One," he whispered. "I wish I could have stopped him."

"It's not your fault," said Betty. "There's nothing you can do about it." Her tears came faster. "But I—I'm scared."

"What are you scared of?" Will asked.

"Everything is going to be different now," said Betty. "Mr. Bromley is—I know he's your father, Will, but he's cruel and frightening."

Will stared at the ground. "I know," he murmured.

"And Martha's hands are so old," Betty wailed, "and so slow. What if he finds out? What if I make another mistake? I can't be dismissed, Will. I have nowhere in the world to go, nowhere. What will I do?"

"I'm sorry," said Will. "I don't know what to say."

The gentleness in his voice made her tears dry up. She wiped her eyes on her apron and managed a smile. "Maybe you don't have to say anything," she said. "I feel better just for talking to you."

Will's smile echoed hers. "So do I."

They sat in silence for a few minutes, listening to the wind howling through the branches. A few stray wisps of snow blew past them, spattering on their clothes.

"You're right," Will murmured. "Everything *is* going to be different. All of our things will be brought here, and we'll be living in London instead of the countryside."

Betty raised her head. "Well, maybe there will be one good thing about the change, won't there?"

Will smiled. "I still have to go to school, you know, but you'll see me every weekend and every holiday now. It's not a long journey by train. I heard Father telling Mama about it, saying that I have to come home on the weekends so that I can learn to run an estate, as he puts it."

"We'll be able to see each other every week?" Betty asked.

"Every week!" said Will. "And not just at Christmas holidays either, but in over Easter and in summer."

Betty grinned.

"You're right," said Will. "There *is* one good thing about all this." He smiled. "You know, Betty, there are plenty of boys to play with at school, but you're my only true friend."

"You're my friend, too," said Betty.

"We just have to be careful." Will's smile faded. "*Very* careful. If Father catches us together..."

"He won't," said Betty.

Will smiled. "I hope not." He slipped down from his root. "I had better go back inside before I'm missed, but I'll see you tomorrow, Betty."

Betty smiled. "I'll see you tomorrow."

She watched him go, brushing through the branches and disappearing into the snow toward the front of the house, the entrance for people who could drink from china cups.

It was still a miserable Christmas, but perhaps Will could be her Christmas miracle, and perhaps he was enough.

Chapter Seven

Four Years Later

Betty tasted the gravy, pressing the delicious, savoury sauce against the roof of her mouth as it trickled over her tongue. For a second, she was distracted by the rich, meaty flavour, and her stomach rumbled.

Pay attention, Betty! she chided herself. It was not quite salty enough for Harold, and sweat broke out on her palms at the thought of what would have happened if she had failed to taste it. She added another half-a-teaspoon of salt, stirred it thoroughly and hurried to tip it from the saucepan into the elegant china gravy boat.

"What's that smell?" said Martha suddenly. She sat on a stool in the corner of the kitchen, her uniform draped shapelessly over her shrunken frame.

The acrid stench of something burning rose from the oven.

"Oh, no!" Betty cried, still busy with pouring the gravy.

"I'll get it." Martha struggled to her feet.

"Martha, no! Your hands!"

Betty abandoned the gravy and wrested the oven open, then pulled out a tray of roasting vegetables. Two onions on the end were blackened, but she breathed a sigh of relief. The others were still all right; she would be able to serve them to the many guests at the party upstairs, its music filtering dimly down to the kitchen.

Martha flopped onto her chair as Betty set out the vegetables and turned back to the gravy. "My poor darling," she murmured. "You should be getting paid like a cook, not a mere kitchen-maid. You do the work of both."

"Nonsense, Martha," said Betty nervously. "No one needs to know about this."

Annie looked up pointedly from the floor, where she was on her hands and knees, scrubbing.

Martha sighed. "I never thought I'd be a burden on you."

"You're not a burden," said Betty sharply. She set the gravy boat down and turned to the vegetables.

"You're only sixteen," said Martha softly. "You shouldn't have to do the work of two people."

"I help too" said Annie indignantly.

"You do, dear," said Martha. "I'm just saying—"

Betty slammed down the vegetable tray. "What does it matter who does what?" she cried. "All that matters now is that we must keep Mr. Bromley happy for today, or we'll all be in hot water!"

Her cry rang through the kitchen, and Martha reeled back as though she'd been slapped.

Betty took a deep breath, trying to hold back the terror and exhaustion that turned to anger so easily, but it was difficult when every muscle in her body ached, when her throat was dry and parched, when her stomach felt shrivelled and sunken with hunger.

"Betty Evans!" Mrs. Coswick cried.

Betty flinched. She hadn't seen the housekeeper coming into the kitchen, and shame made her toes curl.

"You shall not raise your voice in my kitchen!" said Mrs. Coswick, her chin held very high.

Betty stared at the housekeeper, her eyes sunken, her face gaunt with worry. "I'm sorry, Mrs. Coswick."

"Behave yourself, child," Mrs. Coswick spat, "or you may find yourself in a great deal of difficulty."

She swept out of the kitchen, and Betty hung her head. Her exhaustion hung on her back like an immovable weight, slowly crushing her into the ground. It felt impossible to move. It felt barely possible to breathe.

"Betty?" Martha whispered.

It took all of Betty's strength to raise her head. For a moment, the world spun around her, and she clutched the edge of the table to keep from falling. The moment passed, and the ground was firm under her feet again.

"I'm sorry for shouting," said Betty tightly. She arranged the jacket potatoes neatly around the roast peacock. "Annie, could you wash the saucepan for me? I'll need it to make the caramel for dessert."

"All right," said Annie, rising from the floor.

Betty stumbled to the pantry for sugar, but she felt Martha's eyes on her all the way across the kitchen.

~ ~ ~ ~ ~

Betty staggered into the servants' hall, barely taking in all the pale faces turned hopefully toward her as she carried a pot of hot food. From the gardener to the butler to the stable lad, they were grimy and silent, desperate for the supper that arrived after everything was done, when it was already late into the night.

"Where's Victor?" Betty asked tiredly.

"He's still upstairs," said the butler, "serving. I'll relieve him as soon as I've eaten."

"Just serve the food, please," the gardener begged. "I'm famished."

Betty cringed inwardly as she set the pot down in the centre of the table. "It's only chicken and rice, I'm afraid."

A chorus of protest rose from the servants.

"More rice than chicken, too, I'd expect!" the ostler burst out.

"I'm sorry," said Betty.

The housemaid shook her head. "This would never have happened in Mrs. Bromley's day."

Betty longed for the suppers they had had when she was a little girl: the hearty beef stews, the thick slices of bread and butter.

"Can't you just make us decent food, girl?" the gardener demanded, disgusted at the pile of rice in his plate, a few bland strips of chicken draped over it.

"It's not her fault, Ben," said Martha sharply. "She can only work with what she's given, and Mr. Bromley makes the budget tighter and tighter every month when it comes to our provisions."

The complaining settled down to a generalized grumbling, and Betty found the wherewithal to spoon up her own food and sink down into her chair. Even the action of lifting her fork to her lips felt laborious. She was chewing a mouthful, almost too exhausted for that simple action, when Victor burst into the servants' hall.

"Victor!" said the butler. "I'm not—"

"Who cooked the potatoes?" Victor cried.

Betty's heart dropped through her belly. The servants' hall went deathly silent. Her mind flashed through all the steps she'd taken in the kitchen, of salting the potatoes, rubbing them with butter, slipping them into the oven. The burnt onions…

She *had* tested the potatoes for doneness. Hadn't she?

"Who did it?" Victor whispered, his face pale.

Martha stirred beside her, and Betty had to rush to speak before she did.

"I did," Betty croaked.

Martha stared at her.

Victor's mouth turned down at the corners. "Mr. Bromley wants to see you in his study," he said. "At once."

The wave of exhaustion that washed over her was even greater than her terror. The thought of the stairs from the kitchen alone was enough to make her want to scream. Instead, Betty managed to rise to her feet.

"Betty, I'll go," said Martha.

Betty ignored her. She stumbled after Victor, her feet numb, her legs aching as he led her up the stairs and down the long, dark hallway. The pretty paintings were gone, replaced by imperious portraits of men with serious faces and cruel, dark eyes. Old weapons hung on the walls, and ugly tapestries.

Victor stopped outside the heavy oaken door of the study. "I'm sorry," he whispered to Betty, then pushed the door open and stepped inside.

"Miss Evans to see you, sir," he said.

It took Betty a few seconds to stir her legs to movement. She shuffled into the study, a great, dark room, all the lamps behind the desk so that she had to squint up at the imposing form behind it. Harold's chair seemed unnecessarily high, high enough that he loomed over her even sitting down.

"Did you cook those potatoes?" he growled.

Betty stood still, shivering. "Yes."

Harold rose. He moved around the desk, his fists clenched by his sides. The moustache twitched with fury.

"They were underdone," he growled. "The guests hardly touched them. They were like rocks at the centre."

Betty opened her mouth.

"Do not speak," Harold hissed.

Betty shut her mouth and hung her head, shaking.

"You have humiliated me, child," Harold snarled. "You have made me a fool in the eyes of my esteemed guests, people so prestigious that you are not worthy even to see their faces."

Betty squeezed her eyes shut, her heart galloping in her chest. He was going to dismiss her. He was going to make her homeless, here in the heart of winter.

"I should dismiss you for this," he growled.

Betty opened her eyes, feeling a brief moment of relief. It died when she saw that he was holding a cane in his hand, even though Harold did not walk with a stick.

"Hold out your hand," he snarled.

Tears stung Betty's eyes. In the four years that Harold had been their master, she had seen many servants retreat to the kitchen sobbing, their hands red and covered in ugly welts. Betty herself had avoided that fate.

Until now.

Harold growled the words between gritted teeth. "Hold. Out. Your. *Hand*."

Betty inhaled and raised her hand, palm up, shaking uncontrollably.

"Hold it still," Harold snapped.

It took all of her courage not to move as he raised the cane and brought it down in a brisk, business-like motion.

The hard surface smacked across her palm. Numbness, then pain, blossomed through her hand. She bit her lip hard, but did not cry out.

Harold's moustache twitched, and a terrible glint of pleasure came into his eye. He raised the cane and hit her again, then again, and then again. Each blow drove her skin against the small bones of her hand. Each blow made her bite down harder, until blood trickled into her mouth from her torn lip, but she knew better than to flinch.

Five hard blows later, Harold finally lowered the cane. "If this happens again," he said, "you will be dismissed."

It took Betty a few moments to find her voice. "Yes, sir."

"Get out of my sight." Harold turned away.

Betty clutched her wounded hand to her chest and stumbled down the hallway. It was only when she reached the kitchen that she allowed herself to fall to her knees, keening and sobbing with pain, her hand throbbing as she clutched it in her lap. It was almost impossible to clench her fist. How would she wield a mop and broom, a carving knife, a spoon and ladle? How would she cut bread, knead dough, grip a heavy tray coming out of the oven?

It was impossible, but that was the way of the world. For a mere servant girl, it was as cold and hard and unyielding as the kitchen floor upon which she knelt.

~ ~ ~ ~ ~

Betty held her hand, bandaged with a scrap of old rag, close against her chest as she stirred the vegetables that would be made into soup for dinner. It still sent regular pangs of pain through her wrist, but this was the one time of day when she felt that no pain could touch her.

She set down the spoon and placed a lid on the pot, glancing for the umpteenth time at the clock on the wall. Finally, finally, the hour hand had ticked past two. Harold would have gone up to bed to rest, as would most of the guests in the house this close to Christmas Eve. It was the best time of day, the only time of day that was anything except drudgery and pain.

Betty slipped out of the quiet kitchen and peered into the garden, slow and cautious despite the fact that Harold's "prestigious" guests would not be caught dead this near to the servants' entrance. She saw nothing, and it was a pleasant enough day that the gardener had been able to shovel a path. The walk to the old pine—looking more like an undecorated Christmas tree than ever with snow dusting its branches—was easier than usual.

Squeezing between the branches had grown more difficult in the past few years. They snagged on her widened hips, and she crossed her arms in front of her chest to protect it. But when she squeezed through to the middle, there was the same sense of shelter, the same peace.

And the same boy perched on the root, although these days perhaps he was not a boy at all; he seemed more and more, to Betty, like a young man. He could no longer swing his legs where he sat. Instead, their gangly length folded awkwardly. His curls were shorter now, his jaw far more square, shaved clean. There was a strength to his cheekbones that had not always been there, making it almost impossible to look away from them, but nothing would ever change his eyes of Christmas tree green.

He brightened. "Betty!"

"Hello, Will." Betty smiled, her first real smile all day. "I'm so glad you came. I'm sorry for not coming yesterday."

"Oh, I couldn't be there either. I had to be primped and powdered and squashed into my best clothes."

Will pulled a face, looking for a second like the carefree boy she'd known before his grandmother died.

Betty laughed, but feebly.

Will's brow furrowed as she sat opposite him. "What happened to your hand?"

Betty had fabricated a lie to make life easier for him—a believable one, too; she'd burned herself on a hot pan, she'd tell him—but she hesitated just a moment, and a storm gathered in Will's eyes.

"Tell me it wasn't Father," he snarled.

Betty hung her head.

Will sprang up from his seat, his fists clenched by his sides, and marched around the tree. His cheeks were pallid with fury.

"I'm sorry," Betty whispered.

"*You're* sorry?" Will whirled to face her. "Oh, Betty, my love, what in this world do you have to be sorry for?"

"I don't know," Betty wailed. "Everything." She burst into tears.

Will was beside her then, wrapping an arm around her and pulling her close to his chest. Betty didn't know if it was proper or not, but she didn't care; all she knew was that he was warm and his heart thudded with reassuring depth and rhythm when she leaned her head against him.

"Betty, you've done nothing wrong, nothing in the world," Will murmured. "Please never let anyone make you believe you have, especially not my father." He held out his hand. "Let me see."

Betty tremulously raised her throbbing hand and laid it in his palm. Will wrapped both his hands around it with soothing gentleness.

"I'm sorry," he murmured. "This should never have happened. I—I don't understand my father, not at all."

73

"We both know he does the same thing to you and your brother," said Betty softly.

Will's shoulders sagged, and he did not deny it.

"I wish there was a way to stop him," he said quietly. "I would if I could, but it's like stopping a storm at sea."

"The only thing we can do is to weather it," said Betty, "you and I." She flexed her fingers, squeezing his hand lightly despite the pain.

Will's eyes found hers, and he finally smiled. "Papa won't be the master of this house forever, you know," he said, "and then everything will be different. *Everything*."

"I wish it could go back to the way it was when Mrs. Bromley—your grandmama, I mean—was the mistress of the house," said Betty.

Will looked away, a pink flush creeping into his cheeks. "Oh, I think they will be better someday, when this house is mine," he said.

The warmth of the strange and lovely promise in his words made Betty's heart flutter in her chest, and she didn't know what to say. But perhaps, in that sacred space underneath the tree, she didn't have to say anything. Perhaps there were no words.

Chapter Eight

Olive Hilton tried her best not to make any noise, but it was extremely difficult to crouch behind the rosebushes in her full hoop dress. A twig snapped noisily under the hem, and she held her breath, but the voices underneath the pine tree soon started talking again.

"I wonder what it's like to look forward to Christmas," said Will softly.

His voice was smooth and velvety, and it had a musical lilt to it that made Olive close her eyes and sigh with pleasure, and for once there was no pretence to the gesture. She was so much luckier than poor Clementine, her older sister. Mother and Father had chosen Lionel Earl as her suitor—an appalling, lumpen, smelly young man whose fortune nonetheless amounted to thousands of pounds a year. Olive wasn't sure that all those pounds would have tempted her into marrying him, but she knew that Clementine, like Olive, had had no choice.

At least the husband that Mother and Father had chosen for Olive was a pleasant one. Father disliked Will—he called him vapid and cowardly—but Olive thought he was lovely and gentle, unlike so many of the other young men his age.

Will had only one flaw. He was disloyal.

"I've always dreaded it. Father wants everything to be so perfect, and it worries everyone, especially poor Mama. Now, after Grandmama died on Christmas Eve, well…" Will sighed.

"I understand," said Betty.

Olive's hands clenched into fists. That hateful little hussy! She couldn't fathom what Will saw in her. She was the plainest girl Olive had ever seen, and stupid too, and worst of all, she was *poor*. Will had to know that he would never be able to court her, not really.

It didn't sound as though he understood. "Maybe things will be different for us someday."

Us. The word made Olive grind her teeth.

"Oh, yes." Betty laughed. "Maybe one day there will be roast goose and presents and a Christmas tree."

"None of that matters to me," said Will. "Not unless there's love under the Christmas tree, too."

Love. The word fell on Olive's heart like acid, and she could listen to no more. She ripped her dress from the rosebushes, no longer caring who heard her, and raced across the snow, sobbing and tripping over her skirts. By the time she reached the front steps of Bromley House, she was a mess, tears rolling through her powder, snow covering her skirt.

She wanted nothing more than to run upstairs and fling herself down on her bed to weep, but as she ran through the entrance hall, a sharp voice rang out.

"Olivia Jane Hilton!"

Olive stumbled to a halt like a horse wrenched by the bit. A shiver ran down her spine, and she stood trembling, clutching her skirts, suddenly and acutely aware of every single one of her imperfections. The slight tear in one petticoat, making its edge trail on the ground. The leaves in her curled hair. The snow covering her dress. She feared she even had mud on her shoes, although perhaps it was frozen, given all the snow. Olive knew nothing of mud.

The voice blew through her like a cold wind. "Where have you been?"

Olive felt sick. She blotted her tears away with her hands, summoned all of her courage and turned around slowly, trying to compose her face as well as she could.

Mother stood in the hall behind her, perfect and poised in her beautiful dress, her impossibly tight corset, her expression of absolute superiority over all she surveyed. Especially over Olive.

"I was in the garden, Mother," Olive enunciated carefully. "I felt that a walk would be most bracing."

Mother's eyebrows drew down. "Then pray tell, why are you in such a dreadful state?"

Olive lied quickly and effortlessly. Fear had taught her how, ever since she was a little girl. "I tripped on a loose paving stone and fell into the rosebushes." She held out her muddy toe as proof. "That—that is why—"

"Hiltons do not stammer!" Mother shouted. Her voice echoed around the entrance hall.

Olive inhaled slowly. "I beg your pardon, Mother. That is why I am weeping. I was startled."

Mother's eyes narrowed. "What were you doing, walking without an attendant? Do you have no grasp of the protocols that I have done my utmost to teach you since your childhood?"

Olive's cheeks flushed, but she felt relief. Walking without an attendant was a far lesser crime to eavesdropping, in Mother's mind. "I do apologize, Mother. I could not find my lady's maid anywhere."

"That wretched girl," Mother snorted. "She shall be caned for this. And you should, too. You are lucky that your hands must be pristine for the Christmas dance if you are to continue to interest young Mr. Bromley." Her eyes were suddenly two bolts of fire, slicing through Olive. "You understand that you are still to interest him, do you not?"

Olive nodded nervously. "Yes, Mother. I do, Mother."

"Good. Because if you do not marry William Bromley, you will find yourself ruined," Mother growled. "Your only hope is to marry well. Bromley is as well as a girl like you can hope to marry. Do you understand?"

Olive hung her head, tears pricking the corners of her eyes. "I understand, Mother."

Mother gathered her skirts and swept from the room, her lady's maid following her like a silent shadow. Olive exhaled slowly, feeling only a slight tinge of guilt for the punishment that would certainly be inflicted on her ever-attentive maid, who was sitting in her chambers at that very moment, totally unaware that Olive wasn't taking a nap.

Nothing mattered except escaping the household of her mother and father. Will was her way out, unless Betty got in the way.

Olive would have to make sure that she did not.

~ ~ ~ ~ ~

78

Betty grabbed a rag and used it to seize the hot knob of the oven door. She pulled it open, releasing the savoury aroma of roasting goose into the kitchen. It made her mouth water instantly, and she wondered vaguely how many hours it had been since she'd had breakfast—white had been porridge with no milk or sugar. Six? Seven? She didn't know, and at that moment, she didn't have time to care.

"Martha!" she called, slamming the oven door.

Martha looked up from where she was painfully stirring the glaze on the stove. "Yes, darling?"

"Please don't do that. You're only harming your hands," said Betty, as gently as she could. She seized the spoon from Martha and whisked the glaze briskly, wincing at the sight of burned specks in the sauce from stirring too slowly. "Would you keep an eye on the goose for me?"

"All right, darling." Martha sighed and shuffled over to the oven, where she sank down on a three-legged stool and stared dolefully at nothing.

Betty felt a pang of regret for the sharpness of her tone, but there was no time to worry about that now. The glaze was ruined, and it was due to go up in just a few minutes. She donned oven gloves to pick up the cast-iron pan and hastened to the scullery to dump its contents in the sink, but it was already filled with dirty dishes.

"Annie!" Betty barked, the hot pan starting to burn through the oven gloves. "Annie, where have you gone?"

Annie appeared from the pantry. "Right here, Miss Betty."

"Hurry and clear out these dishes. Now!" Betty yelled.

Annie turned pale at her tone and scrambled to fish pots, pans and ladles from the sink.

Betty's hands stung as she dumped the disastrous glaze into the sink, then scrubbed the pan quickly with salt and cool water. She ignored the searing pain on the back of one knuckle where she'd pressed it against the pan for too long as she hastened back into the kitchen, dumped the pan on the stove and restarted the glaze from scratch.

"I'm so sorry, Betty," Martha whispered.

"Please watch the goose, Martha." Betty's hands quaked as she scrambled to put together the ingredients for the glaze. She poured them into the pan and whisked rapidly, feeling only a tinge of relief as it started to come together, this time without the ominous black flecks.

She took the glaze off the stove and hurried to fetch the dried parsley from the pantry for cutting as a topping. The pantry was in chaos, herbs piled hither and thither, and Betty tried not to think of the way it had looked years ago when she had been a kitchen-maid to an organized cook. There was no time to organize it now; there never was. She shoved boxes and jars out of the way until she found the dried parsley and hurried into the kitchen with it.

"Miss Betty!" Annie stepped out of the kitchen. "Don't we need the silver gravy spoon?"

Betty cursed under her breath. "Hurry and wash it for me, Annie."

"Yes, Miss Betty." Annie disappeared into the scullery.

Betty finished chopping the parsley and poured the glaze over the roast vegetables ever so carefully, making sure not to spill a single unsightly drop. She took fistful of parsley and sprinkled it over the vegetables, already resting on the beautiful serving dish that rested on a silver tray.

"Victor!" she yelled. "You can start taking up the main course!"

The footman appeared at the bottom of the stares. "Not a moment too soon, Betty," he said. "They were starting to look impatient."

"Hurry, then," Betty barked. "Take the side dishes first. Martha, is the goose ready?"

Instead of responding, Martha let out a strangled sob. The sound reverberated down to Betty's toes. She whirled around and saw that Martha was doubled over, a rag lying on the floor by her feet, clutching her hand. A burn blister swelled on her index finger.

"Martha!" Betty ran to her side. "Are you all right?"

"My stupid hands!" Martha sobbed. "My stupid, stupid hands!"

The roast goose no longer smelled so perfect, and Betty's heart stopped.

"Annie!" she shouted. "Fetch Martha a handful of snow for this burn!" She gently moved Martha out of the way, grabbed the rag and slid the oven door open. The goose bubbled inside under its crispy skin, a skin that was two shades too dark.

"Oh, no, no," Betty whispered. She grabbed oven gloves and pulled the goose out of the oven. Its juices hissed and sizzled as she put it down on the table. There were no black parts, but the goose looked shrunken in its skin, not juicy and bursting like it would have done if it had been cooked to perfection.

And perfection was the only standard good enough for Harold Bromley.

Victor thundered down the stairs, and Betty realized she didn't have time to do anything to make this right. She slid the goose onto a serving dish, tossed a dismayed handful of parsley over it and slid it across the table to Victor.

Victor hesitated. "Is it—"

"Take it," said Betty, "before you get in trouble for it."

Victor turned pale at the thought. He grabbed the tray and hustled up the stairs.

Betty closed her eyes and took a deep breath. Had she averted disaster? She closed her hand, still feeling the throb where Harold had hit her, and could only hope that she has.

When she opened her eyes, she fixed her smile firmly back in place and turned to Martha. "Oh, Martha, I'm so sorry about your hand."

Martha clutched the snow that Annie had brought her. "It's all right, darling." She swallowed. "Let... let's get started on pudding."

She smiled bravely, and Betty returned the smile. But she knew what they were both thinking.

How much longer could either of them keep this up?

~ ~ ~ ~ ~

Christmas Eve was almost over, and Betty couldn't be more relieved.

She scrubbed the kitchen table, working a brush over the worn wood, her arms aching with exhaustion. This was kitchen-maid's work, and she'd already done the work of a cook all day, but who else was to do this? She was painfully aware of Martha watching her from her stool by the fire, where she held her bandaged hand to her chest.

"Almost done," she said, as cheerfully as she could.

The sounds of music and laughter echoed dimly through the floors. Betty checked the pot on the stove. It contained a watery beef stew, the best she could do for Christmas dinner for the servants with what Harold had given her, and she knew they would be unhappy with it, too.

Her stomach rumbled as she stirred the stew. Though it contained mostly gristle floating in a watery sauce with lumps of turnip and potato, Betty couldn't wait to eat. Her head felt faintly dizzy with hunger.

The sounds from upstairs grew louder.

"Is someone shouting?" Annie asked.

A moment later, Betty heard it too.

"Father! Father, *no*!"

Her insides tied themselves in a knot. The voice belonged to Will, and the clattering footsteps were heading downstairs. Toward them.

"Father, this is most improper!" Will shouted.

"*You're* being improper," Harold snapped back.

Betty's heart turned cold inside her. Harold had found out about their spot beneath the Christmas tree, about the long Sunday afternoons they spent talking there, about their friendship that had gone on for eleven years.

"Please, Father!" Will cried, his voice even closer now. "Wait until tomorrow. If only—"

"Be silent, boy!" Harold raged.

The kitchen door banged open, and their master towered at the top of the stairs, his eyes alight with fury. A gasp ran through the kitchen. The master, in the *kitchen*! It was almost incomprehensible. Martha's cheeks were white with fury at this breach of the rules that governed every respectable house in London.

"Sir!" she cried, leaping to her feet.

Will appeared behind his father, breathless and dishevelled. "Come on, Father," he begged. "Let's go back to the party."

"No!" Harold shook off his son's hands. "I have had it. I have *had* it with the absolute incompetence and total disrespect shown by my servants!"

His yell ripped through the room, and everyone froze, silent and pale as they stared at Harold. Betty wanted to run away and hide, to curl herself up into a tiny ball inside the pantry and disappear. Instead, she stood silent, head bowed, trembling, and it took all of her courage to do so.

"That goose," Harold hissed, "that goose was meant to be the centrepiece of Christmas dinner for my family and friends. I wish to enjoy my Christmas. Do you hear? That is what Christmas is *for*—luxurious enjoyment. Yet you have robbed me of that with your utter stupidity!"

He screamed the last word, and everyone flinched.

"Now I am going to ask this only once, and I expect to be told immediately, or there will be consequences for everybody." Harold looked around the room, malevolence glittering in his eyes.

Betty found the courage to raise her head and looked pleadingly at Will. Tears filled his eyes, and he held up his hands behind his father's back. A gesture of total helplessness.

"Who cooked that goose?" Harold hissed.

Betty stepped forward, but before she could speak, Martha's voice cut through the silence. It was pure and strong and steady, the way it had been on that fateful Christmas when Betty had almost frozen to death on the street.

"I did," Martha said.

Betty whirled around. "Martha!" she cried.

Martha held up her trembling, bandaged hands, but there was no fear in her eyes as she looked at Harold. "I cooked the goose," she said, loud and clear.

Harold's eyes narrowed. "It was overcooked," he hissed. "Practically burned." He stepped forward, his voice rising. "How dare you shame me in front of my guests?"

His sentence ended in a yell, punctuated with the slap of bone against flesh as he struck Martha across her cheek. She gasped and fell back, raising a hand to the reddening welt on her face.

"Father!" Will cried.

Harold whirled around, his hand raised threateningly. "Boy, if you do not hold your tongue, you will be taught a lesson!" he raged.

Will cowered, raising his hands over his head as though to protect himself.

Harold spun back to Martha. He seized her arm and pulled her close to his face, his sneer twisting his features.

"You are dismissed," he hissed. "Get out of my sight, and never come back."

Martha's head snapped up, colour bleeding from her face.

"No!" Betty cried, stepping forward.

"Silence!" Harold roared.

Martha met Betty's eyes and gave a slight shake of her head. A tiny movement, but it stopped Betty in her tracks.

"Go," Harold growled. He shoved Martha away. "Get out of my house."

"But sir—" Betty cried.

"One more word out of you," Harold thundered, "and you will be dismissed, too."

Betty froze. Will shook his head rapidly, his eyes wide with fear, and for his sake she said nothing. What could she say? What could she do to stop this?

Martha stood very straight, her useless old hands dangling by her sides. "I'll tell you this, sir," she said, with all the dignity she could muster. "Your mother would be ashamed of you."

The colour bled instantly from Harold's face. He opened his mouth, as if to give a retort, but could think of none in the face of Martha's stern eyes. She did not give him the opportunity to think of one. Instead she turned and climbed the stairs with utmost dignity.

"Where are you going?" Harold yelled.

"To get my things, sir," said Martha, not looking back at him. "And then I will be gone."

Chapter Nine

Martha had made good on her promise. She was gone.

The kitchen felt bigger, emptier, yet at the same time the walls were falling in on Betty, crushing her where she stood at the kitchen table, peeling potatoes. When Harold had dismissed his cook, he had not thought of who would cook Christmas lunch, but Betty knew that the consequences would be dire if the peacock (goose was too common for Christmas Day itself, in Harold's eyes) was not roasted and stuffed and the mince pies were not made and the Christmas cake was not presented. Harold would go looking for someone to blame. She knew she was already on thin ice.

Thin ice. It was a good expression for the way she felt, staggering across a frozen wasteland, hearing the ominous crackle of the ground beneath her feet. As though the very earth was conspiring to shatter underneath her, plunging her into deadly cold.

She tossed a fistful of peelings into the slop bucket and reached for the next potato. Her hands trembled with weariness. Floors above, music had begun.

The feast was starting, the feast for the people who drank from the china cups, for people who were not Betty.

She wondered where Martha was. She wondered if Martha was cold or scared or alone. The thought made her heart bleed within her. She had fallen on her knees and begged, *begged* Martha to stay as she packed her things last night. She had pleaded with the only mother she knew to stay. Looking back, she knew now that that had been foolishness, the railings of a frightened heart.

Martha could never have stayed, but now Betty was alone in the world, except for Will.

She glanced at the clock, wondering if they would have any time together that day. Likely not. Christmas luncheon went on for hours, followed by guests, and of course Olive Hilton was here. Just to add insult to injury.

Betty's hand slipped on the knife, and she winced as the tip pricked her palm. She set down the potato and rinsed her hand at the kitchen sink, blinking back tears. Such a tiny hint of pain, yet her world was so filled with agony that this latest injury seemed insurmountable.

She leaned against the sink, taking deep breaths, her eyes screwed tight shut, and then heard it. The purposeful thudding of footsteps, and Will's voice, pleading.

Her eyes snapped open. No... surely not. Surely this couldn't be happening all over again.

"Father, this must be a misunderstanding!" Will cried.

Betty hurried into the kitchen. Annie, Mrs. Coswick and the other maids were already there, wide-eyed and worried.

"Get out of my way, William," Harold barked.

William staggered down the stairs backward, as though trying to fend off his father, but Harold was inexorable.

He swept to the bottom of the stairs and raked the assembled servants with a single imperious glance, and there was cold fury in his eyes.

Mrs. Coswick stepped forward. "Mr. Bromley! This is most improper!"

"Be silent!" Mr. Bromley bellowed. He held out a hand. "Come now, Miss Hilton. Tell them what you told me."

Olive shuffled down the stairs, the picture of the miserable victim. Powder ran on her cheeks as it mixed with tears. Her eyes were red, her head bowed. Betty had never seen Will look openly disdainful before, but he glared at her now.

"Are you sure you didn't simply misplace it, Olive?" he asked.

"Oh, Will, how can you be so cruel?" Olive cried. "I know I did not. It was my grandmother's comb, all set with pearls, and I know my maid took it from my hair last night and left it upon my vanity. And now it's gone! One of you has taken it." She jabbed an accusing finger at the servants, her eyes fixed on Betty. "I know you have!"

Mrs. Coswick stepped forward, her hands shaking. "Have you spoken to your lady's maid about it, Miss Hilton?"

"Of course she has. Don't take us for fools, old woman," Harold snapped. "The maid was the first person whose room was searched, and the comb was not found. Rest assured she was nonetheless punished for her carelessness." His hands tightened on his cane so that it creaked.

Betty's heart stuttered.

Mrs. Coswick swallowed. "The… *first* person whose room was searched?"

"Yes." Harold turned to the stairs. "Jeremy, get down here! Don't be lily-livered like your brother."

Will shrank back as his younger brother, a blockish, brutish young man, stomped down the stairs. There was a menacing glimmer in his eyes.

"Come, Jeremy," said Harold. "You and I will search the rooms. You too, Mrs. Coswick. And if we do not find the comb in any of the servants' rooms, I will have no choice but to hold you accountable."

"Search our rooms! *Yourselves*?" Mrs. Coswick cried. "Sir, that is most—"

"I don't care for impropriety!" Harold screamed, veins sticking out on his neck. "I care for returning that comb to my esteemed guest!"

He stormed up the stairs, Jeremy close behind, and Mrs. Coswick ran after them, clutching her skirts.

"Will, what's happening?" Betty cried.

"Oh, Betty, I'm so sorry." Will stumbled toward her, stared at the maids, then stopped. "I don't know what's going on."

"None of us took her comb, Master Bromley," Annie quavered.

"I know that. It's simply misplaced somewhere of course! But Father—" Will raked his hand through his hair. "I'm so sorry."

Annie turned to Betty. "Betty... Mr. Bromley's eyes. Is he... he seemed... well... he seemed quite mad."

Betty shivered.

"I can't say I disagree with you, Annie," Will murmured.

Thunderous footsteps again, and everyone in the room cowered. Harold burst down the stairs, clutching aloft a silvery comb studded with pearls, and Betty's heart sank. She knew that yet another of her friends—her family, by now—was going to be thrown into the dark and cold.

"You!" Harold roared, and strode toward Betty.

Will cried out and tried to step between Betty and Harold. His father slapped him aside, the blow ringing across Will's cheek with easy violence that sent him reeling.

"Will!" Betty cried.

"*You*!" Harold grabbed her arm, pain shooting through her forearm where he clutched it.

Betty screamed, and Harold cuffed her on the back of her head, rattling her teeth.

"You stole this from one of my guests," he hissed, his breath smelling of eggnog. Far too much eggnog. "You brought shame on my head, on my *family*."

Betty leaned away, sobbing. "I didn't, sir. I swear, I didn't. I'm just a kitchen maid. I don't even go to Miss Hilton's room."

"How did this comb get into your cupboard, then?" Harold bellowed.

Betty froze. "I don't know!"

She looked past him at Mrs. Coswick, whose mouth turned down bitterly. The housekeeper shook her head, disappointment in her eyes.

"Sir, I swear, I didn't take it!" Betty cried.

"Tell me how it ended up in your room, then!" Harold roared.

Betty saw the triumph in Olive Hilton's eyes, and suddenly she knew exactly how. But what could she say? What defence was there to make against a girl like her?

"Jeremy, send for the police," Harold barked. "She will hang for this!"

"Hang? No!" Betty screamed. "Please, sir!"

"Oh, Master Harold," said Olive, with saccharine sweetness. She stepped forward, doe-eyed. "Please, don't do this to the poor girl. She's quite simple, as you can see. I don't want to see her die."

"She cannot get off scot-free, Miss Hilton," Harold snapped.

"I understand that, sir." Olive hung her head demurely. "Only please don't call the police. I can't bear to have her harmed." She pressed a hand to her chest. "You know how tender-hearted I am, sir."

Harold gnashed his teeth, then turned to Betty. "You see? This is what separates the higher classes from people like you. This noble young woman has saved your life today." He shoved her away, and Betty staggered against the table with a cry.

"I didn't do it!" she yelled, her hands clenching suddenly into fists as a jolt of rage ran through her.

"Get out of this kitchen," Harold thundered. "Get off my property! Now!"

Betty hesitated. A wild fury roared in her at this injustice, and for a moment she wanted to scream at him. But when she looked into Will's eyes, the fury turned instantly into cold, clutching terror and pain.

The look on Will's face was not anger. It was something a thousand times worse: disappointment.

He didn't believe her.

A choked sob tore from Betty's lips. She could not bear another instant in this house, this house with Will and his broken heart. She dared not even go upstairs to get her things. She just turned and bolted from the servants' entrance and into the snow, ignoring the cold that tore at her face, at her dress, at her spirit.

~ ~ ~ ~ ~

If it was not for the bitter cold, Betty's courage might have failed her.

She stood with her arms wrapped around her body, shivering as she gazed up at the grim, austere building, all high walls and narrow windows, unwelcoming and severe. Despite the tattered, badly made Christmas wreath hanging on the door, the building still frowned down at her, as though disapproving of her very existence. Thin lines of snow lay on all its ledges, and the snow was still coming down hard and fast, piling on Betty's arms, soaking through her hair.

A fresh gust of wind drove her forward two steps on the pavement outside the building. She couldn't stay out here, she knew. There was no Martha Evans coming to save her this time. That night, she'd exhausted her lifetime supply of Christmas miracles, she was certain.

If she stayed out here, she would die. It was that knowledge alone that drove her up to the door.

She knocked twice before hearing footsteps in the hallway. The door swung open, and a round-faced man with a jolly red glow in his cheeks chortled at her. "Merry Christmas!" he said, and tried to close the door.

"No. Wait!" Betty stopped him. "Please, sir."

The man gazed at her. "What do you want?"

"Please, sir," Betty repeated. "Is this the workhouse?"

The man chuckled. "Of course it is. What else would it be?"

"All right." Betty swallowed. "I… I would like to come in."

The man's eyes raked her, from her soaked and tattered uniform to the way she hugged herself, desperately missing her coat.

He sighed. "Matron won't be happy."

"Please, sir," Betty whispered. "It's so cold."

The man shrugged. "All right." He turned and walked away, leaving Betty alone to shut the door behind her, sealing herself in a narrow hallway that smelled of socks.

The light was insufficient here, and she froze for a second, feeling as though she'd been trapped in a coffin. Then she heard a burst of laughter down the hall and stumbled gladly in that direction.

She glimpsed a doorway outlined in light, and then another door crashed open to her left. A sour-faced woman glared down at her from an imperious height.

"You're the new intake?" she barked.

"Yes, ma'am," Betty quavered. "I'm—"

"This way," the matron snapped.

She turned and strode down the hallway, which was bleak and grey and only seemed to get longer as Betty walked, as though she had been trapped on the inside of a nightmare. She scuttled after the matron with a pounding heart. The woman didn't look back at her, not once, and Betty did not dare to speak. The echo of their footsteps rang around the hallway, almost drowning out the sounds of the workhouse around them, which warped into terrifying yells and screeches in the fevered quagmire of Betty's frightened mind. She thought she heard mad singing and screams of agony and bursts of wild cackling. But the echo of their footsteps was too loud for her to be sure.

The matron stopped and pushed open a door to their right. "In there," she ordered.

Betty shuffled into a tiny, cold, windowless room. It contained a tin tub, and copper pipes swarmed over the walls, ending in two taps. Shelves covered one side, containing bags— each with a paper label—and endless folded rows of faded, striped clothing.

The overwhelming urge to flee seized her, but it was too late. The matron slammed the door behind her and went over to a rickety desk in the back of the room.

"Why do you need relief?" she droned.

Betty swallowed. "I was a kitchen maid, but I was dismissed this morning, and—and I don't have anywhere else to go."

The matron scribbled in a book with a blunt bit of pencil. "The admissions board will see about that."

"What?" Betty squeaked.

"It's Christmas Day. I'm in no mood for trouble," the matron barked.

Betty hung her head. "No, ma'am. I don't intend to give you any."

"Strip," said the matron.

Betty blinked. "I beg your pardon?"

The matron gestured with her pencil. "Take off your clothes, girl."

Betty froze. "*All* of them?"

"How else do you think you're going to bathe?" the matron snapped. "Come now."

She went to the bath and opened the taps; one steamed and one did not, and the matron opened the steaming one so that only a faint dribble trickled from it.

"I don't have all night," the matron snapped. "Strip or you'll miss supper."

Tears filled Betty's eyes. Slowly, she peeled her uniform from her flesh, which goose-pimpled and shrank in the cold air. The matron stared at her with cold, unfeeling eyes until she had taken off every petticoat and undergarment. She all but fled into the bath, desperate for that tiny semblance of privacy, but there was none. The matron seized a brush and scrubbed her violently, offering her much less regard than she'd seen the stable boys give to horses while grooming.

The matron whisked her uniform away while she was drying herself in the frigid air. Instead, Betty was presented with an ugly dress, striped white and grey.

"Wh–what is this?" Betty whispered.

"Clothing, and you'll be grateful for it," the matron snapped. "Get dressed."

Again, she did not turn away as Betty pulled the ugly dress over her head. It sagged from her shoulders, utterly shapeless, the hem threadbare. Betty wondered how many other hapless women had worn it before she did. It changed something in her the moment she donned it; she felt reduced, inferior. Marked by her own helplessness.

She was given shoes, stockings and a shapeless bonnet.

"This may," the matron barked, and strode away.

Betty shuffled after her, allowing tears to tumble down her cheeks. She stared at her feet, enclosed in heavy grey stockings and shoes that did not quite match, and barely noticed the ambient noise changing around her until the matron said, "Take a plate and don't cause any trouble."

The matron vanished, and Betty raised her head. She was standing in a bleak grey dining hall with windows painted shut, but nonetheless admitting a whistling draft that stung Betty's cheeks with its cold. Snow beat against the window, and rows upon rows of women in dresses exactly like Betty's sat at the long tables.

In comparison with the utter greyness of the room, the futile decorations here and there were a pathetic attempt at cheer that only served to heighten the utter misery. Scrawny wreaths, dotted with wilted holly berries, hung from the walls. There was no tree, and the bunting hanging from the main table had been badly crumpled.

Betty stumbled over to the table, where a handful of bony young women served the food. She grasped a tin plate and held it out wordlessly to the women.

"Christmas dinner tonight!" said one of them. "Isn't it lovely?"

They dropped food on her plate, and Betty blinked at it. A piece of roast chicken with a blob of congealed gravy. A single roast potato, and a slice of Christmas cake, dry and containing nowhere near the normal amount of raisins.

"Thank you," she mumbled, and took the first empty seat she could find.

No one spoke to her. Betty took a bite of the roast potato, which was cold and lacking salt. It smeared around the inside of her mouth, tasteless, and she struggled to choke it down despite her ever-present hunger.

She couldn't stop thinking about the look in Will's eyes, the utter disappointment. The pain. How could he believe that she would steal?

It took her a few moments to realize that she was being watched. An older woman sat across the table from her, staring at her, slack-jawed and pale. Her eyes were piercingly blue, and lines of worry and trouble marked her forehead and mouth.

Betty met her eyes and offered her a smile. The woman went on staring, her gaze making Betty uncomfortable. She looked away, feeling that the woman must be infirm in some manner.

She stared at her meagre Christmas dinner instead, and it was everything but lovely.

Chapter Ten

One Year Later

Betty winced as the tip of the needle probed her thumb. She could hardly believe that her thumb had any feeling left at all anymore, but this time, the needle bit deep. A bead of blood glistened on the pad of her thumb, and Betty sucked it hastily before it could draw any attention from the matron.

She glanced around nervously for the dreaded matron. The work hall was huge; dozens of women sat on uncomfortable benches, variations on the ugly striped dresses, shirts and trousers lying on the scratched tables in front of them as they sewed. There was not a word of conversation in the room, but only the muted rustle of fabric and snap of thread.

Betty exhaled. The matron, Miss Paulson, was on the far side of the room, glaring at one of the youngest women. The girl was no older than fourteen, and she cowered, sniffling, under the matron's angry glare.

"Miss Paulson!" a strident voice cried across from Betty.

Dismay filled Betty's heart. It was Mrs. Brooks again.

The woman who had stared at her so intently on her first night in the workhouse was not so infirm after all. Despite her grey hair and wrinkled face, Mrs. Brooks was much younger than Martha, and her mind and hands were both as sharp as could be. Betty knew; she had been on the receiving end of both.

"Please, Mrs. Brooks," she hissed.

"Miss Paulson!" Mrs. Brooks cried.

The matron strode along the tables toward them, her face thunderous, yellowed eyes narrowing. "If you don't hold your tongue—"

"I beg your pardon, Miss Paulson," said Mrs. Brooks sweetly, "but Miss Evans here is ruining this dress. I thought you should know."

Miss Paulson's eyes snapped in Betty's direction with predatory focus.

"I pricked my thumb! I only pricked my thumb." Betty held it up, but she moved too quickly. A fatal droplet of blood splashed from her thumb and onto the dress she was busy with, staining a tiny circle in the fabric. Her heart plummeted at the sight.

Miss Paulson's face twisted into an ugly sneer. "Look at this mess!" she screamed.

"I'm sorry, miss," Betty wailed. "I'll—I'll make it right. I can—"

"You wretch," Miss Paulson hissed. "You're too lazy or crooked for anyone to hire you, so you come here and expect everything to be handed to you on a silver platter. Now when you're expected to work to earn your keep, you continually destroy everything you touch!"

Tears stung Betty's eyes. She had no idea how to tell Miss Paulson that her continual misfortune was anything but coincidental. Mrs. Brooks' triumphant grin reminded her of a dozen tiny incidents: bits of rope stolen when they were picking, laundry dropped in the dirt when they washed, always blamed on Betty.

"Please, miss," she whispered.

"To the laundry room!" Miss Paulson thundered, pointing.

Betty's heart quailed at the thought of labouring with her hands in that scorching water, the air thick and stifling in the dark cellar beneath the workhouse. "Oh, please, miss, I've just done my week's rotation there. I—"

"*The laundry room!*" Miss Paulson screamed.

Betty winced, terrified at the thought of what would happen should she dare to disobey. "Yes, Miss Paulson. Right away, Miss Paulson," she whimpered.

As she scampered from the sewing room, she spared the time to glance over her shoulder. Mrs. Brooks watched her go, her eyes glittering with triumph.

Betty had no idea what she had done to earn this woman's ire, but she did know this: she had been Mrs. Brooks' target since she arrived at the workhouse almost a year ago. She wished she knew why, or that Mrs. Brooks would simply stop.

~ ~ ~ ~ ~

Will sipped delicately at the tea that his valet had brought him. The young man, Victor, was a composed and quiet sort, always out of the way. Sometimes Will wished that Victor would pluck up the courage to strike up a conversation with him. Perhaps it would allay the piercing loneliness that had plagued him ever since—

No. Will flinched away from the thought. No, he wasn't going to think about that. About her.

He sipped his tea and leaned back against his duck-down pillow as Victor fussed around the room, turning down the covers, laying out Will's clothes.

"I'm going riding this morning, Victor," said Will, "first thing."

"Yes, sir." Victor hesitated. "Do you not have breakfast with Mr. Bromley, sir?"

Will sighed. "I appreciate the reminder, but I'm going to do my best not to attend."

Victor inclined his head. "I understand, sir. I will set out your riding things."

"Thank you." Will closed his eyes, consumed with thoughts of how he was going to avoid his father today. It had become his singular quest since last year, when he had finished school and begun what his father called "training in business". So far, it had mostly consisted of Father shouting at him and Will stumbling around in bewilderment or feeling a fool at meetings as his father criticized him endlessly.

It was tempting, at times, to wonder where it had all gone wrong with Father. Will remembered a cuddly, laughing, happy man when he was a little boy. Of course, that had been before his own older brother died when he had gone ice skating with Father, back when Father used to do fun things. Perhaps Father had never forgiven himself.

Or perhaps Father had never forgiven Will for not being James.

Curtains hissed as Victor drew them open. Welcoming any distraction from the heart-breaking memory—Christmas fourteen years ago now—Will opened his eyes, and his heart squeezed.

The plane tree outside his window extended a branch directly across his view. Watching a pair of robins build their nest and raise their young on that branch had been one of Will's few pleasures that summer. Now, the leaves were all gone, and every twig was edged in sparkling frost. Beyond the tree, the gardens of Bromley House shimmered under their curtain of ice.

Will sat bolt upright, almost spilling his tea. "What date is it, Victor?"

Victor drew the curtains on the other window. "The fifth of November today, Master Bromley."

November fifth. It was nearly winter, Will realized.

Almost Christmas.

The memory of last Christmas made tears sting his eyes. He blinked them back, the way he had so much practice doing in front of his father, and suddenly he couldn't hold back the memories anymore. Not just the appalling images from last Christmas: the silver comb in Father's hand, the look of utter horror in Betty's eyes, the dizzying realization that she, his friend, his beloved, had taken something that wasn't hers.

No. The memories that now assailed him went far deeper than that. He remembered long summer afternoons sitting beneath the pine tree, laughing. Wintry mornings meeting her with hot tin cups of tea. The cup now in his hands wobbled, and he set it abruptly on the nightstand, but tea still slopped over the wood.

"Master Bromley?" Victor asked worriedly. "Are you all right, sir? You've gone very pale."

Will tried to squeeze out a word, and could not. All last year, he had dreaded leaving school. It was his only sanctuary, despite the bullies and the harsh professors and the dull food. It was a place where his father never came.

His only consolation had been the same thing in which he'd trusted ever since Grandmama died: that he would have one friend in the world, and it was Betty.

He'd even looked forward to last Christmas, knowing he could see Betty every day. But she had betrayed him and now he was stuck here with Father, bearing the brunt of his abuse almost alone. The horror of it sank down around him, making the walls feel as though they were falling in. Will struggled for breath against a chest that felt like it was being crushed. What was the point of this, of anything? How would he ever escape Harold?

"Sir!" Victor cried, grasping his arm.

Will blinked, suddenly able to take a breath. "I'm all right, Victor. Don't be worried. I'm quite all right."

Victor stepped back, his forehead creased in worry. "Should I send for the doctor, sir?"

"No, no." Will waved a hand. "I'm all right." He sighed, his soul shrivelling within him. "You know, Victor, you may set out my formal clothes instead. I won't be riding this morning."

"But why not, sir?" Victor asked.

Will shrugged. "What does it matter?" he murmured. "What does any of it matter?"

Victor stared at him for a few long moments, the colour draining from his face. Then, suddenly, the footman buried his head in his hands.

"I can't do it!" he cried. "I can't do it anymore, sir!"

"Victor!" Will jumped out of bed. "What on Earth is the matter?"

Victor swayed, sobbing into his hands. Fearing he would faint, Will grabbed the valet's arm and guided him into a chair. "Victor, speak up, man! What is wrong?"

"I've been lying to you, sir!" Victor cried. "I've been lying to you all along!"

Will stared at him. "What are you talking about? You're the most honest man I know. It was you who found the comb in—" He couldn't say Betty's name. "That was why Father made you my valet instead of just a footman, because you'd proven your integrity."

"Oh, sir, that's what you don't see," said Victor. He raised his head, his cheeks ashen. "I *didn't* prove my integrity that day. In fact, I did quite the opposite."

Will's blood turned cold. "What are you talking about?"

Victor squared his shoulders. "Sir, I know that what I am about to tell you will cost me my work, but I can hide this from you no longer. You have been so terribly kind and so very good to me—better than anyone has ever been in my life, except perhaps for Betty."

"Don't say her name," said Will. "I beg you."

"Oh, sir, but this is why I must tell you what truly happened that day." Victor swallowed. "Betty did nothing wrong. It was… it was me."

Will sat down sharply on the edge of his bed. "Victor, I plead you, do not tease me. My heart is already in ribbons over Betty. I have barely succeeded in burying what happened. I cannot dig it up once again."

"Sir, I am not teasing. I'm finally telling you the truth," said Victor. "I do not deserve your kindness, but for your own sake, please hear me out."

Though the fire crackled in Will's room, he felt suddenly very cold, as though the November frost had crept into his bones. He shivered and wrapped his arms around himself. "All right. Tell me."

Victor took a deep breath. "I won't try to defend my actions, sir, but I'll tell you everything and maybe you'll understand." He hung his head. "I dared not say anything to anyone, fearing that your father would smell weakness on me, like a wolf smelling blood, but do you remember Verity?"

"The parlour-maid?" Will asked. "Who dropped the glass?"

"That's right, sir," said Victor.

"What happened to her?" said Will. "I never saw her after that."

"Mr. Bromley dismissed her, sir, and she fell into a terrible life. She was—" Victor blushed. "She was part of a disreputable establishment, sir. I tried to get her out of it, because truth be told, I was in love with her. But the, ah, the lady who ran the establishment would not let her go. She demanded to be paid for her, as though she could be sold."

"So you were desperate for money," said Will softly.

"It still does not excuse what I did," said Victor. "That Christmas Eve, Miss Hilton came to me."

Will straightened. "Olive?"

"That's right, sir. She was weeping and pleading for help, and I... I listened to her. She told me she would give me a whole pound—the price of Verity's redemption—if I did something for her."

Will swallowed. "You mean..."

"Yes." Victor met his eyes. "Miss Hilton gave me a pound to hide her comb in Betty's room. Betty did nothing wrong, sir. It was me."

Will covered his face with his hands. His heart pounded wildly in his chest, and emotions flooded through him, so hot and fast that he could barely feel them, let alone recognize them.

"I'm so sorry, sir," Victor wailed. "I know it was a terrible thing, but oh, please, don't destroy yourself because of something I did. I've watched you pine away after Betty and it breaks my heart. But she did no wrong. None! I don't care what you do to me, but you have to know the truth!"

Will raised his head and extended a hand. Victor flinched back, raising a hand as though he expected to be struck. Instead, Will seized Victor's right hand and wrung it.

"Victor," he said, "for once in his life, my father was right. You *are* a man of integrity."

Victor pulled his hand away. "Sir! Didn't you hear what I told you?"

"I heard you perfectly," said Will, "and I know you felt that you had no choice. You did it for love, Victor; I can understand that. I would have—*should* have—done something foolish for love a long time ago. Don't be afraid; I shan't tell Father."

Victor's shoulders sagged. "Oh, thank you, sir. I'll never forget your grace, I swear it. I'll make it up to you. Tell me what I can do. Anything!"

"You can help me to find Betty," said Will. "I want to see her before Christmas."

Victor's jaw clenched. "Yes, sir," he said. "I will." He bustled off to prepare Will's clothes.

Will walked to the window and gazed out at the frosted grounds of Bromley House. Suddenly the world seemed to be wrapped in a glorious diamond. It held colour again. It held life.

Will hardly cared that he'd found out Olive had tricked him. He had always known she was a schemer; it did not surprise or upset him. But to know that Betty was the woman he'd always trusted she was, the girl with the golden heart, the childhood friend who had blossomed into his one true love—that was everything to him.

Now he needed, for once, a Christmas miracle. He needed to find her.

~ ~ ~ ~ ~

Sleep was a fitful thing in the workhouse. Betty lay curled on her side, her knees pressed against the cold wall, the hard edges of her sleeping pallet digging into her hip and shoulder. A large, snoring woman sprawled beside her, a new intake, the smell of stale drink still thick on her breath. Betty could only hope she wouldn't vomit. There was no room for her, but she had already lost three fingers to frostbite, so the workhouse had had no choice but to take her in. And she had chosen to collapse on Betty's sleeping pallet.

She drifted in and out of a restless slumber, dreaming of Mrs. Brooks. The woman chased her through her nightmares, shrieking, those blue eyes wild. Sometimes her face seemed to blend with another, this one more youthful.

Betty startled awake, sweating, from a nightmare where Mrs. Brooks' fingers grew longer and longer until they grabbed Betty's face and suffocated her. Her movement made the snoring woman groan and roll over, giving her even less space on the pallet.

Exhausted, Betty chided herself for her silly dreams. Mrs. Brooks had been in the infirmary for two days now. She had rest from her during the day; now if only her tortured mind would give her rest during the night.

The only advantage of the snoring woman was the warmth that radiated from her body. Betty pressed against it, shameless in the face of the November cold that crept up from the floor and slipped so easily beneath the threadbare blanket, and drifted to sleep once more.

This time, her sleep was dreamless. The next thing she knew was a cold, hard grip on her arm.

"Wake up!" Miss Paulson barked loudly. "I told you to wake up!"

Betty's eyes snapped open. Had she overslept? Missing the morning bell was an offense punishable by caning. She sat up, bewildered, but it was still absolutely dark except for the flickering light of a nearby candle. It was held by a wide-eyed woman; one of the nurses from the infirmary. Betty had seen her creeping around from time to time.

"What?" she spluttered.

Her first thought was that the drunken woman had died beside her. New intakes did at times, and it always appalled her. But the woman stood nearby, loose-lipped and angry, her eyes red in the candlelight.

"Miss?" Betty croaked.

"Go with the nurse," Miss Paulson ordered. "Hurry."

Before Betty could ask why, the nurse had turned and hustled out of the room. Betty jogged after her, uncoordinated with sleep, staying as quiet as she could. The nurse immediately took a set of bare iron stairs leading up to the infirmary floor.

"Ma'am? Ma'am!" Betty cried. "Where are we going? I'm not ill."

They reached the top of the stairs, and the nurse turned to stare at her, candlelight flickering over her face. "One of the patients is on her deathbed," she said, "and she asks for you."

Betty blinked. She had occasionally seen this nurse drag other women from their beds to say a final goodbye to family members dying in the workhouse, often husbands or children from whom they'd been separated for years.

She had no idea why Miss Paulson allowed it, since it was against workhouse rules; perhaps because Miss Paulson, like Betty, was afraid of this nurse with her big dark eyes and her huge, hooked nose.

"Who?" Betty asked.

"Rose Brooks," said the nurse.

Brooks? Betty froze in place. Why did the woman choose her dying moments to terrorize her?

"Hurry," said the nurse. "She is not long for this world."

Betty found herself stumbling after the nurse into the infirmary. It was a large room, brutally lit with gas lamps, illuminating the steel bedframes and cheap sheets and the emaciated bodies of the workhouse inmates that came here to die. For this was no place of healing. Betty knew it, felt it in her bones as she stepped inside.

"Here," said the nurse.

Betty had expected Mrs. Brooks to be the raging monster of her nightmares. Instead, when they approached the bed, she was a shrunken woman, her eyes closed, her cheeks sunken. She was not that old, Betty realized suddenly. She had to be several decades younger than Martha. Certainly not yet forty.

"Mrs. Brooks," said the nurse, with surprising tenderness. "Miss Evans is here to see you."

Mrs. Brooks did not open her eyes. "Miss Evans," she whispered. "It always felt strange that they called you that."

The nurse drifted away, leaving Betty all alone by the bedside of her dying nemesis.

Mrs. Brooks turned onto her back and opened her eyes. They were fevered pits in her face, and her breaths were laboured, wheezing. Her lips were ringed with blue.

"I was going to take this secret to my grave," she whispered. "But now that the grave is at my feet, well..." She had to pause and pant for breath.

Betty waited, shivering.

"The priest... the last rites." Mrs. Brooks swallowed. "I fear death. I cannot deny it. Maybe it's too late for me... but I must do what I can... to be sure I end up on the right side of... of eternity."

"I don't think it's ever too late," Betty whispered.

"Perhaps you are right." Mrs. Brooks sighed. "Stupid, sweet girl. Oh, how I wish I'd never done what I did to you."

"I forgive you," said Betty.

Mrs. Brooks barked a laugh that ended in an agonizing cough. "Forgive me! You don't know what I did to you, child." She wheezed. "You think you forgive me for... for petty transgressions... for bullying. No, Betty. I did far more than that." She paused. "I destroyed your life."

There was no chair beside the bed. Betty shifted her weight, worried by the ravings of this mad, dying woman.

"You don't believe me," Mrs. Brooks whispered, "but do you remember your governess?"

A jolt of ice ran down Betty's spine. "I do. Miss Parker. She abandoned me in a market square a few days before Christmas when I was only five."

"Yes. Yes, she did." Mrs. Brooks groaned with mortal pain. "Oh, the foolish, foolish girl! I didn't think. I was as spiteful then as I am now. Oh, what a life to regret!" Her words dissolved into coughing.

Betty swallowed hard. *I didn't think*, Mrs. Brooks said. Suddenly the youthful face of her nightmares appeared in her mind with greater clarity.

Suddenly those blue eyes were far more familiar than they should be.

"Mrs. Brooks," Betty croaked. "Were you…"

"Yes," said Mrs. Brooks. "My maiden name is Parker. I'm the one who left you there, Betty."

Betty's knees buckled. She sat down sharply on the edge of the bed, her chest so tight she could barely breathe.

Mrs. Brooks—Miss Parker's—eyes were unfocused now, glassy. Her words tumbled out in chaotic fragments, broken up by ragged, gasping breaths.

"It was your father… such a fine man… so handsome… Your mother was forced to marry him, you know. She never loved him… but I did… oh, I did! We were… so happy together… He loved me, even though I was just a governess… well, I thought he loved me. Fool! Foolish girl! Fool!" Miss Parker dissolved into terrible, wet, sucking coughs that sounded like they were tearing her lungs apart from the inside.

"Then your mother found out. Oh, the harpy! He… he said… he was going to leave me… dismiss me. I heard them… arguing in the study. I knew I couldn't… couldn't stop him." She groaned, her eyes rolling in her head, skeletal hands clutching the sheets. "Fool! *I was the one who loved him.* But no… he was going to leave me… for *her.* I had to… I had to hurt her. Get her back. The thing… the thing she loved the most… was you."

A sob tore loose from Betty's mouth. She clapped a hand over it. Her mother had loved her. She had had a mother, and she had been loved.

"So… I got rid of you… and I left." Miss Parker coughed again; this time, it seemed hardly any air reached her lungs at all. "But I had no references… When your mother told my parents what I did… they threw me… out. I had nowhere to go but the workhouse. The moment I saw you, I knew.

You… you're the spitting image… of your grandmother… on your mother's side. And now I'm here." The last word was a whisper. "Dying."

Betty covered her face with her hands and wept for the little girl in the snow, for the mother who must have sought her so desperately, perhaps even a little for the stupid Miss Parker.

"Forgive me," Miss Parker whispered, the last syllable drawn out in a breath that went on for too long.

Betty's head snapped up. "Miss Parker?" She grabbed the woman's arm. "Miss Parker!"

But the arm was limp in her hands, the eyes sightless, the mouth hanging open.

"No!" Betty screamed. "No! Miss Parker, wake up! Wake up!" She shook the body, and the head lolled uselessly. "You didn't tell me who you worked for. You didn't tell me who my mother was. Tell me. Tell me!"

But Miss Parker's face remained frozen in a last grimace of spite, her confession a last dagger sunk deep into Betty's flesh.

Chapter Eleven

Will walked as quickly as he dared on the icy pavement. The wind was brutal, ripping at any scrap of flesh it could find between the scarf he'd bundled around his face, both for warmth and for anonymity. If Father ever found out was he was doing…

He pushed the thought away. Father would never find out; he was away on business for the next week, and this was the best chance Will had to find her.

He clutched a piece of paper in his hand, and as he hastened down the slippery pavement, sleet drove into his eyes, making it difficult to read. But he had no need to see the words on the paper. Victor had written the address for him last night.

"My brother is a porter there, sir," he had whispered, handing Will the paper. "He said he thinks she might be there."

It was a vague clue, but after nearly two weeks of constant searching, it was the only thing that Will had. He clung to it, the paper worn and creased from his constant fondling.

Finally, the workhouse loomed ahead. Sleet drove against its windows and melted miserably on its ledges. At the sight of that cold, hard, heartless building, Will's heart faltered within him. Had his Betty really been there for almost a year? How had her tender heart survived such a place?

Maybe it hadn't. The fear of that possibility drove him to walk faster.

He slithered his way up the steps to the narrow front door and knocked. A porter opened it; a young man with the same ginger curls as Victor.

"I'm looking for a girl," Will burst out. "Betty. Betty Evans. Is she here?"

"You mean an inmate, sir?" said the porter.

"Yes. Yes! Is she here?" Will asked eagerly.

The porter shrugged. "I don't know, sir. I only carry things and open doors."

Frustration bubbled in Will's chest, but he held it back. "Can you find out?"

"Miss Paulson might know. She's the matron." The porter grimaced. "But she's not always happy about visitors."

Will drew himself up to his full height, perhaps for the first time in his life. "I am William Bromley," he said, "heir to the Bromley estate, and I wish to speak to her at once!"

The porter's eyes widened, and he scrambled off. Will had never wielded his name like a weapon before, and he didn't like it, but he would do anything to see Betty again. Even this.

A few minutes later, a bitter woman with a cruel, lined face came to the door. Her eyes widened.

"You *are* Master Bromley," she said. "You were in the paper with your father."

"Yes, ma'am." Will inclined his head. "Please, I was hoping you could help me."

Miss Paulson glared at him. "I have important things to do, Master Bromley."

"I know that," said Will, "and I'll also inherit the Bromley estate." He glanced around the workhouse. "I believe a generous benefactor may make your lives easier someday…?"

Miss Paulson swallowed. "What can I do for you, sir?"

"I'm looking for a girl called Betty Evans," said Will. "Is she here?"

Miss Paulson sneered. "Pah! She's here. Troublemaker of a girl!"

Will's heart leaped. "Bring her to me, please. At once. I am taking responsibility for her. She will no longer have to remain in the workhouse."

He expected Miss Paulson to be contrary, but instead she threw up her hands. "Good riddance!" she cried. "I will begin the paperwork at once."

~ ~ ~ ~ ~

Betty stood quaking in the long, cold hallway. She hadn't seen this hallway—the one leading to the front door—since she was admitted to the workhouse, and the air here seemed thick with misery. She wondered how many tears had been shed in this hallway as helpless paupers found themselves dragged into this life.

Now, though, Betty was going the other way, and she had no idea what was happening. Her workhouse uniform had been taken away from her, and she now wore the uniform with which she'd been admitted. It hung shapelessly on her body, far too big after a year of workhouse fare, and she shivered in it.

"Please. Miss Paulson," she quavered. "What manner of a gentleman was it?"

The matron shoved some papers into her hands. "Oh, you'll find out soon enough," she barked.

All Betty had been told was that a gentleman had come for her. The possibilities threading through her mind were all terrifying. She knew that sometimes men came to get young people from the workhouse for menial work, like children for chimney-sweeps, or girls for worse.

Much worse.

Terror gripped her so tightly that she could barely shuffle after Miss Paulson as the matron led her to the front door. The porter stepped forward, and the door was flung open, bringing in a gust of freezing air and a blast of sleet that prickled harshly against Betty's face. She blinked it from her eyes and looked up at Will.

The sight of him made her knees tremble. For a wild moment, she thought she'd died of fear, and was looking into the heaven of his face. But then he gasped, and he was real flesh, standing in front of her, his eyes still the same green as a Christmas tree, his hair blowing in the wind.

"Betty!" he cried, and held out his arms.

Betty cared nothing for what was proper. She could only stumble into them, and he was holding her, smelling of pine needles and roasting chestnuts. He was shaking, perhaps even sobbing, as he held her, and it was so easy and natural for her arms, too, to surround him.

When he stepped back, his cheeks were wet. The workhouse door was closed; they were alone on the windblown porch.

"Oh, Betty, Betty!" he cried. "I'm so glad that I finally found you."

"What are you doing here, Will?" Betty whispered.

"I came looking for you," said Will. "Betty, I'm so sorry. I should never have believed all that rubbish about the comb. Victor told me everything—how Olive paid him to hide it in your room. I can't believe I would ever have thought that you would steal. Oh, Betty, can you forgive me?"

"Yes." The word spilled from Betty before she could think. She had no need of thinking; all she needed was right here. "Of course I forgive you."

Will hugged her again, fiercely, and Betty leaned into him. It was the type of embrace that said he would never let go.

~ ~ ~ ~ ~

Wind rattled the windows, and even though she'd been here a month now, part of Betty still braced herself for the blast of cold air that was sure to come howling in. But no cold came. These windows were new and sturdy, and the glass was immovable as a great gust of snowflakes drummed against it.

Betty sighed with relief. She set the teapot on the little coal stove and stood close to it out of habit, warming her hands over the cast iron even though she was wrapped in a warm wool coat and the little kitchen was far from cold.

She checked on the rabbit pie in the oven; it was turning nicely golden on the top. Even now, it was difficult to believe that that pie was for her.

Betty pottered around the kitchen, trying to decide what to do with herself, but confronted with the startling reality that there was nothing to do. The floors were clean, the grate in the single fireplace was polished to a fine shine, the laundry was done, and she had swept and dusted every corner of the flat. She stood in the doorway between the postage stamp of the kitchen and the little living room, which had just enough space for two armchairs, the fireplace, and a bookshelf, containing two books and an old wooden top with its colours nearly worn off.

There was not much else to the flat—a bedroom with a narrow bunk and a tiny washroom—but Betty felt pride swelling in her heart as she looked at it. It had been a long time since anywhere felt like home.

The lid of the teapot clattered, and Betty poured herself a cup. It was a china cup, too, somewhat out of place against the ordinary furnishings of the flat, but Will knew what it meant to her. Then she selected a book from the shelf—one of Will's first readers from school—and settled in the armchair with her tea. She read slowly, sounding out the longer words, but it felt good.

It felt like something Martha would be proud of.

Her eyes strayed to the other book on the shelf. It was a great, thick volume with cheap pages, and the title was difficult to read, but Betty had seen the words so many times by now that she knew them well. *London Directory, 1883.*

She set the reader aside and took the heavy book into her lap. She'd marked her page with a ribbon—it was near the middle—and she flipped it open, tucked the ribbon into her hand, and looked down the rows of names.

Mr. Puttergill

Mr. Jones

Mr. Cox

Mr. Petersen

Mr. Halstead

Most of the names were gibberish to her, but she knew exactly what she was looking for: *Evans.*

She was three pages in, running her finger down the rows of names as she worked to decipher them, when a knock at the door interrupted her. Betty's heart leaped.

She set the directory on the arm of her chair and sprang to her feet, a grin already on her face as she hastened to the door.

She flung it open, and Will stood on the landing, his hands tucked into the pockets of his greatcoat. His hair was windblown and dotted with snow, and his cheeks nipped bright red by the cold, but his smile lit up his eyes.

"Hello, darling!" he said.

"Will!" Betty longed to embrace him, but they had long since agreed that though their courtship was secret, it would still be as proper as possible. She stepped back. "Please, come in. I'll make you some hot tea."

"Oh, that would be marvellous. Thank you, Betty," said Will.

He wiped his feet before coming in and took off his coat and mittens to hang on the hooks by the door. Betty bustled about, taking the biscuit tin and putting the teapot on to boil. In a few minutes she had arranged some biscuits and scones on a plate and made his tea exactly the way he liked it.

She brought the tray to the small table between the two armchairs, and Will took the tea gratefully, wrapping his hands around the cup. "Ahhh. That's better. Thank you."

Betty grasped a poker and stirred up the fire, then added a few bits of wood. "I didn't think I would see you today, the weather being what it is."

"It's Wednesday, darling. I wouldn't dream of not coming," said Will seriously.

Betty smiled. "You haven't missed a Wednesday or a Saturday since you brought me here."

Will shrugged. "That's what I promised, and I intend to keep that promise."

"Thank you," said Betty.

"Does the tenement still suit you well?" Will asked. "I know it's very small, but I had to use as little of my allowance as possible, to be sure that it was kept secret."

"Oh, Will, you ask me every time I see you, and I'll give you the same answer every time." Betty laughed. "It's warm and dry, and I can keep it as I please. It's everything that I need and I will never be able to thank you enough." She smoothed a hand over her new dress; it was one of several, warm and sturdy.

Will shuddered. "I will never allow you to suffer as you suffered again, my love."

"I get to see you again," said Betty seriously. "That's more important to me than anything else."

A flush crept into Will's cheeks, and he looked away shyly. His eye rested on the directory on the arm of Betty's chair. "Have you had any luck?"

"Not yet," said Betty. She sighed. "I'm starting to understand what you said. Almost every person listed here is a 'Mr.', except for those who are 'Doctor'. I hardly know if a widow would be listed at all."

"Neither do I," Will admitted. "But you're only halfway. Maybe you'll still find her in there."

"I can't believe nobody back at the house knows where Martha went," said Betty. "Martha used to talk about her brother Bernie, but you say Mrs. Coswick says she has no idea where he lives, either?"

"None." Will shrugged. "I don't think anyone at the house cares for much anymore, beyond staying away from my father, and I can't blame them."

Betty laid a hand on his arm and squeezed. "I'm sorry."

"It's all right." Will's smile broke like dawn. "You're here. That means everything is all right."

It wasn't entirely true, Betty knew. Despite hours searching through the directory and a month of hunting through marketplaces, she still didn't know where to find Martha. But when she looked into Will's Christmas-tree-green eyes, she could almost believe him. She could almost accept that all was well with the world.

Chapter Twelve

Will's pen flew over the page. He paused only briefly to refill it before he went on in his most beautiful, careful script. It was very different from the casual scrawl he used to write notes to Betty. This was painstaking and cautious; anything less would arouse his father's anger. Even his best writing was likely to do the same, but Will had learned to do everything in his power to prevent an outburst.

He finished the letter and wafted it in front of the fire to dry. It was a simple note arranging a meeting with Lord Graham regarding Father's business dealings with an important trading company, but he knew that his father's standards for such things were exacting. Carefully, he folded it up and placed it in an envelope.

He was about to call for Victor when the door swung open and his valet stepped soundlessly into his room.

"Ah, Victor," he said. "There you are. I was just about to call for you to—"

"Sir." Victor swallowed hard. "Mr. Bromley sends for you."

Will froze in his seat. "I've finished the message," he said. "You can give it to the boy, then tell him that I did as he asked."

Victor had looked better over the past month, ever since he'd confessed what happened last Christmas, but now his cheeks were ashen. "Sir, I don't think it's about the message. Please. He's in his study."

Will rose slowly, trying to keep his hands from shaking. "What is the matter, Victor?"

The valet said nothing. He darted out of the room, and Will followed him down the sumptuous hallway, passing all those hateful portraits of "great Bromleys" in the past, portraits from whom Grandmama was conspicuously absent.

His gut roiled as he walked. Had Father somehow found out about Betty? But it was impossible. Will paid for her tenement cautiously, giving her a shilling here and there, hiding it among the casual spending that Father would easily accept. Had he had Will followed? Surely not. Not even Father was this paranoid. Was he?

The study door swung open, and a lance of terror shot through Will's heart. Olive sat in one of the high-backed chairs at the bottom of Father's desk, her head hanging demurely, the picture of docility as Harold loomed over her. Mr. and Mrs. Hilton stood on either side of her, dressed to the nines, as always. Mrs. Hilton gazed down at Will with a contemptuous sneer on her painted lips, and Mr. Hilton's face was a stone mask.

"William, sit down," said Harold.

Will swallowed. "Good afternoon, sir, ma'am." He bowed deeply. "Good afternoon, Olive."

"Hello, Will," said Olive softly.

Mrs. Hilton did not acknowledge him; Mr. Hilton gave a brief nod.

"I told you to sit down, boy," Harold growled.

Will slunk into the chair next to Olive's.

"Good." Harold steepled his fingers, elbows resting on the desk. Will felt very small with his father and the Hiltons towering over him. "William, Mr. and Mrs. Hilton and I have reached a decision."

Will shot a furtive glance at Olive, who smiled back at him, her eyes wide and triumphant. Terror curdled in his belly.

"You have been allowed ample time to court Miss Hilton," said Harold, "and you have made very little progress in asking for her hand in marriage. Regrettably, it is well known to us all that you are a slothful boy with no initiative and very little brains. However, we still consider that a marriage to Olive would be advantageous to both families. You would thus be able to produce heirs to the Bromley name and Olive would be well set for life."

Will straightened. "Father, if I may—"

"You may not," Harold growled.

Will fell silent.

"Therefore, since you are too inept to handle these matters yourself, we have decided to handle them for you." Harold smiled. "You and Olive will be married on the first available Sunday in January, when Christmas is over."

Will shot upright in his chair. "Married!"

"Indeed," said Harold.

"It is an unusually short engagement," said Mrs. Hilton, "but we are more than ready. I have already had Olive's gown designed."

"A beautiful gown it is, too, Mama," said Olive simperingly.

Mrs. Hilton glared at her. "I should hope so. I have excellent taste."

Will opened and shut his mouth soundlessly, utterly at sea in this preposterous situation. He had long feared that his father was not entirely sane; looking at his glittering eyes now, he believed it to be true.

"Father, don't you see how ridiculous this is?" Will burst out.

Harold's eyes glittered dangerously. "You will do as I tell you, boy. Hold your tongue."

"No, Father!" Will leaped to his feet. "I am not a chip to be bartered with!"

Harold blinked, but Will was just as surprised by his courage as his father. Betty's smile filled his mind, and reckless bravery flooded his veins, hot as fire.

"Neither Olive nor I are part of your business or company. We are human beings!" Will cried.

"I have no complaints," said Olive.

"I am certain you do not," Will raged, "given that it was you who hid your comb in the servants' quarters to manipulate my father into dismissing our kitchen-maid because you were jealous of her beauty."

Olive gasped. "Will! Why would you tell such a heinous lie?"

"Enough!" Harold thundered.

Will cowered, expecting a blow, but in the Hiltons' presence Harold kept his hands to himself.

"I tire of your insolence, boy," Harold snapped. "None of your ridiculous assertions will make any difference. The decision has been made. You will marry Olive in January. You are now engaged; a suitable ring is waiting for you at the jeweller's. You will collect it and proceed forthwith. Do you understand?"

Will stared up into the monster's face, his heart quaking within him. Then, suddenly, it stilled. Betty's face floated in his mind, radiant with love and joy.

"Yes, Father," he said meekly.

"Very good," said Mr. Hilton, drawing a frightened look from Olive.

"I shall go to the jeweller's at once and do as you ask," said Will.

Harold relaxed. "Very well. Go."

Will kissed Olive's hand, unable to meet her eyes, bowed to the Hiltons and went to his room to change into his very best.

He knew exactly what he had to do, and it had nothing to do with going to the jeweller's.

~ ~ ~ ~ ~

The day was unusually nice for mid-December. Betty strolled down the street toward her building, humming to herself and smiling as she admired the decorations on all of the homes she passed. These were ordinary buildings, with twenty families sharing the same floor space as Bromley House, but their paint was not peeling and their inhabitants had the money to buy colourful candles for the windows and wreaths for their doors. Last night's snow had not yet melted, and it crunched under Betty's feet as she walked, unable to hurt her through her thick boots and warm stockings.

Her heart had been heavy when she turned down this street. She had just visited the home of a Mr. Evans who lived three blocks away, hoping wildly that it was still the name of Martha's husband on her own home address, but the young man who lived there had never heard of a Martha Evans before.

Now, though, humming *O Christmas Tree* enough times had brightened Betty's heart. She would find Martha eventually; she would try until she succeeded. For tonight, she had to make a wreath for the front door, so that Will would see it when he came on Saturday. The basket on her arm was laden with greenery, holly, ribbons and wire from the generous allowance that Will gave her.

She climbed the steps of her building, still humming and admiring the mistletoe that had been wrapped around the banisters of the wooden stairs. She was so busy looking at it that she nearly walked into someone standing by her front door.

"Oh!" She stepped back. "I beg your pardon!" Then Betty froze. "*Will?*"

The young man's eyes were alight. He grabbed Betty's arm. "Betty, I'm so glad you came."

"I was at the marketplace," said Betty. "Whatever is happening, Will? You look—different."

He looked more than different; he looked aglow, bright as a Christmas candle in a window.

"I have something to ask you," he said. "Please, let's go inside."

Betty didn't know what was happening, but the light in his eyes made her heart pound with happiness. She unlocked the door and brought him into the warm flat. As she hung up her coat, set down her basket and stoked the fire, she waited for him to do the same and settle into his chair, but he did not. Instead, Will practically danced in place by the door, his smile as wide as the moon.

"Will!" Betty laughed. "You're making me nervous. What is it?"

Will stood still and took a deep breath. Then he held out his hands, and Betty slowly placed her hands in them.

"Perhaps this is unorthodox," he said, "but I believe it is glorious and real all the same, and there is no more time to waste." Suddenly he was down on one knee, and he was taking something from his waistcoat pocket, something small that shone, and Betty couldn't breathe. Her head spun with wild joy and terror all at the same time.

"Betty Evans," Will said softly, "you have been as bright as the Bethlehem star in my life since I was a little boy. Would you do me the honour of becoming my wife?"

Wife. The word resounded through Betty's soul like a clanging gong. All the reasons why this was impossible shot through her mind at once, and none of them seemed to matter at all, not compared with the joy in Will's eyes or the certainty thudding in her heart.

"Yes," she heard herself say. "Oh, yes, Will, yes!"

He threaded a ring over her finger; it was a simple iron band, but in her world it was everything. Then he was on his feet, and he wrapped his arms around her and spun her around and around in the little room until she was dizzy and laughing and the whole world seemed like a glorious dream.

He set her on her feet, and she gazed into his sparkling eyes, happier than she had ever been in her life.

"Oh, Betty," said Will, "I love you."

"I love you!" Betty cried, delighted to at last speak the words that had, in some way, been true ever since she had stumbled upon a kindly boy in the hallway outside the drawing-room all those years ago.

Will laughed. "Then I must ask you something more."

"What is it?" Betty asked.

Will sat down on the nearest armchair, and Betty sank into the other.

"Betty, I have been wanting to do this for a long time," he admitted, "perhaps longer than you know, but I was hoping to allow you time to settle in before I asked this question. Something happened today, something that made it more urgent."

Betty stared. "What?"

"My father is trying to force me to marry Olive Hilton in January," said Will, "and I would rather die than marry anyone but you." He spoke the words with utter seriousness.

"Force you?" said Betty.

Will shook his head. "I told you, Betty, Father is quite mad, and I'm afraid that the Hiltons don't care; all they want is for Olive to marry well. But I shan't marry her. I shall marry *you*." He wrapped her hand in both of his, caressing the thin band on her left ring finger. "So I will ask you one more thing."

"Of course, Will," said Betty. "Anything."

Will's gentle heart shone in his eyes. "Will you marry me *today*?"

Betty did not hesitate. To her mind, there was no reason to. "Of course I will," she said.

~ ~ ~ ~ ~

Their wedding was perfect.

Betty wore a pale blue dress, the one she kept for church on Sundays, and held a bouquet of holly. They went to the little church at the end of the street, where her vicar looked into their eyes and saw no need to ask any inconvenient questions. Nor did he have to; they were both of age.

He called his wife, the gardener and his grown daughter as witnesses, and they sat huddled together in the front pew of the freezing church. As the vicar read from the Bible and spoke their vows, his words rose on a cloud of steam.

The entire church was draped in mistletoe and holly. Wreaths hung from every surface; the altar was decorated with great bundles of verdant greenery. Every candle was lit, bathing the space in golden light, flickering across the great wooden cross that presided over their wedding.

Afterward, Betty remembered very little else of the ceremony, except for the look in Will's eyes. She never looked away from his face, not even as she slid an iron band onto his finger, too.

And she remembered the kiss. The way his lips found hers.

It was something that would be impossible to forget.

~ ~ ~ ~ ~

They emerged into the afternoon light to find that snow had begun to fall. The flakes were fat and white and sparkling, gathering on Will's eyelashes, dusting his shoulders. Betty couldn't look away from his radiant smile as they walked to the gate at the end of the church grounds.

"What will we do now?" she asked as they reached the road.

Will blinked, as though the question had not occurred to him. "I don't know."

"Should we go back to my flat?" Betty asked.

Will's grin widened. "We will, to get your things, but that's for later." He laughed. "You're my wife now, Betty. I'm bringing you home."

Wild joy leaped in Betty's heart. Not at the thought of Bromley House—she hardly cared to see that place again—but at those words: *You're my wife now*. Nothing else mattered compared to that.

Will led her to the nearest thoroughfare and raised his hand for a cab, and they stepped in, giggling and smiling, still dusted in snow. It was Betty's first time in a carriage, and she couldn't stop smiling as it sped through the streets of London, moving faster than she'd ever gone before.

~ ~ ~ ~ ~

Betty had thought that she didn't want to see Bromley House again, but when the cab stopped at the front steps, she felt a sudden pang of nostalgia at the sight of the old place. Her eyes did not go to the beautiful bay windows or the turrets or the many grand wings; instead, she looked in the direction of the kitchens, and the tiny windows beneath the roof where the servants lived, and spotted the dark point of the undecorated Christmas tree peeking out on the other side of the house. It was all edged with white snow, making it look like it should be in a picture book.

Will sprang from the cab and held out his hand. "Come, my love."

Betty giggled. She took his hand and allowed him to help her down, and the cab drove away, leaving them alone at the base of the steps. Betty had never climbed them herself; they were for other people, the china-cup people.

But she was one of those people now, she realized.

Will strode up the steps, keeping a tight grip on her hand, and Betty scrambled after him. He used the great brass knocker to knock on the front door.

It swung open, revealing Victor, looking very dashing in his livery. Will had told her that Victor was his valet now;

Betty hadn't thought she could forgive him for what he'd done, but in this mood she felt she could forgive anyone.

"Sir!" said Victor. His eyes strayed to her. "*Betty*?"

Will chuckled. "It's Mrs. Bromley now, Victor."

"What?" Victor gasped, his eyes darting to Will's finger.

"Let us in, if you would," said Will. "It's freezing out here."

Victor backed away and closed the door behind them as they stood in the grandeur of the entrance hall. Staring up at the giant double helix of the staircase, Betty felt a sudden pang of terror, and she tightly clutched her husband's hand.

"Where is Father?" Will asked.

"He's in the drawing-room, Master Bromley," said Victor, "but I don't think—"

Footsteps on the stairs. They transported Betty instantly to Christmas Day a year ago, the day her world fell apart, and her breaths came in terrified little gasps.

Harold Bromley appeared at the top of the stairs. He paused for an instant, his eyes sweeping Will and Betty. Betty was shaking, but Will stood firm, his free hand clenched into a fist.

"Father," he said.

"What is the meaning of this?" Harold growled.

He approached down the stairs toward them, slinking like a prowling wolf, his eyes absolutely predatory.

Will faced him bravely, chin up. "Father, I wish to introduce you to my wife," he said.

Harold froze halfway down the steps. He stumbled, almost fell, and grabbed the mistletoe-draped banister.

"I beg your pardon?" he spat.

Will did not yield. "You heard me, Father. This is my wife." He tugged Betty forward a step. "Mrs. Betty Bromley."

Every vestige of colour drained from Harold's face. His wild eyes stared at Will from a deathly grey mask, and Betty's heart froze.

"What have you done, boy?" he hissed.

"What I knew in my heart I should do," said Will bravely. "I married the woman I love more than anything in this world, the woman who has been my rock, my sunlight, the firm ground on which I stand."

"That *servant girl*?" Harold shrieked. "You married a mere *pauper*?"

"I married the best person I have ever met!" Will cried. "Grandmama would have been proud. Grandmama would understand!"

Harold all but charged down the steps. Betty let out a small scream as he raised a hand to slap Will across the face, but this time, Will did not go undefended. He seized Harold's wrist and pushed his father back, not hard, but with enough force that Harold stumbled back two feet.

"Father, I will no longer be misused by you," he said. "If you strike me I shall stop you."

Harold stepped nearer. His eyes were wild; flecks of saliva sprayed from his mouth as he hissed his next words. "You will take this woman to the workhouse where she belongs and leave her there, boy. Then you will bring me the name of the idiot who married you, and we will have this marriage annulled at once. No one need ever know of its brief and miserable existence. You will marry Olive in January as you were told. And that will be an end to it."

Will squared his shoulders. Betty gripped his hand tightly, her heart drumming, yet at the same time more proud of Will than she could ever express.

"I will do no such thing, Father," he said. "I have made a holy vow before God to love and cherish this woman until the last throb of my heart, and I shall do it, regardless of what you or anyone else says."

Harold raised a hand. Will twitched, as if to defend himself, but it seemed the elder Bromley had realized that his son was nearly a foot taller than him, with broader shoulders and greater resolve. Instead, Harold pointed at the front door.

"Go," he rasped.

Will hesitated, confused.

"Leave this house," Harold hissed. "You aren't fit to be my son. I wish never to see you again, and you shall not touch one drop of my estate, do you hear me? Your younger brother shall have everything. You were never worthy of my fortune."

Will blinked. Betty could barely comprehend what she had heard.

"*GO!*" Harold screamed, veins popping in his neck.

The door clicked as Victor pulled it open. Harold screamed the word again, foam gathering at the corners of his mouth, and this time Betty tugged at Will's arm. "We have to go, darling," she said. "We have to go."

Will stumbled blindly after her. Harold railed in the great room, shrieking over and go, "*Go! Go! Go!*" until the sounds were less like a human voice and more like the tortured howl of some caged predator.

"I'm sorry," Victor whispered as he shut the door behind them.

Then they were outside, in the cold.

Chapter Thirteen

It was surprising how quickly Betty's hands and arms had become unfit to the realities of manual labour. They ached furiously now as she plodded down the street, her hands tucked into the pocket of her dirty, damp apron after a long day working in a washerwoman's basement. She had only a few meagre pennies to show for the back-breaking day's work. On Monday, the day after tomorrow, she would have to pay the rent, and she had secreted most of the money away. All that her apron pocket contained was half a loaf of bread.

She had been married for a week, and she feared it would be her last week in the nice little flat, unless Will was able to keep a job. He had worked one day at the cotton mill before being dismissed for working too slowly, and one day at the brickyard, but returned with his hands so torn and bleeding that he could barely sleep that night. He'd wanted to go back to the brickyard again the next day, but Betty had seen a job listing for a stable hand at a livery stable nearby, and she talked him into going there instead. Perhaps that work would be gentler on his pampered body.

A troubled sigh escaped her as she touched the edge of the bread in her pocket. It was somewhat stale, and she hoped Will with his refined palate would find it edible. It had taken him three days to grow used to porridge. If he didn't find work soon, that porridge would have to become gruel.

These worried thoughts swirled in her mind as she walked up the street, but they were interrupted sharply by a strain of beautiful music. Betty stopped to look up at the church on the corner—the one in which they'd been married last week. The choir was practicing their carols, and the beautiful words filtered through the wintry night, brightening the dark street punctuated only by starlight and the glow of lampposts.

Sing, choirs of angels
Sing in exultation!
Sing all ye citizens
of Hea'en above!

The voices were loud and jubilant, and Betty closed her eyes and breathed deeply, allowing their hope and joy to fill her soul. She was hungry, tired and cold, and afraid for the future, but she was going home to the arms of a man who loved her fiercely enough to lose everything for her.

There was a new spring in her step as she walked to her building and climbed the many steps, then tried the door. It was unlocked; Will must be home.

"Darling!" she called, pushing it open. "I've brought—"

Her words died in her throat when she saw them: a pair of shoes protruding from behind the kitchen table. Sad, damaged shoes they were, designed for treading lightly on thick carpets instead of work, caked in mud and melting snow, attached to a pair of motionless legs in damp trousers.

"Will!" Betty screamed.

She rushed to Will's side. He lay face-down on the kitchen floor, his eyes closed, hands on either side of his head like he'd used them to break his fall. His hair was dark with snow and slicked down to his forehead; when she touched his arm, it burned against her skin.

"Will!" she cried again.

His eyelids fluttered, and he groaned.

Betty rolled him onto his back, searching for a wound or blood or any sign of why he would have collapsed, but there was none; only a dreadful rattle in his breathing, a sound not unlike the noise Miss Parker—Mrs. Brooks—had made as she lay dying. It scared the life out of her, and when he coughed, it was a terrible, choking rasp.

"Will, darling, my love, please," Betty begged. "Open your eyes."

Will did, but when he looked up at her, there was hardly any expression in them; their green was dull and lifeless, and they were deeply sunken in their sockets.

"What happened, my love?" Betty cried. His clothes were soaked through; she couldn't tell if it was from sweat or snow.

"So tired," Will whispered. "So... tired." He winced, pressing a hand to one side of his chest. "So sore."

He was sick, Betty realized, fever raging through his body. She'd noticed his hoarse voice that morning; he'd told her it was from shouting over the voices of other workers in the stables. Now she knew that he had been lying to protect her. And why would she be surprised that he'd fall so ill so quickly? He had spent his life in warm rooms, eating sumptuously and never straining himself unduly; manual labour, cheap food and chilly days had already taken their toll on his pampered constitution.

"Let's get you to bed," she quavered, pulling his arm over her shoulders. "You'll feel better with—with a bit of bread—and maybe some tea." She struggled to hold back her tears.

Will swayed against her, damp and sweating, as she supported him into the bedroom. He sat on the edge of the bed, breathing hard, his body unresisting as Betty stripped off his wet socks and coat.

"I'm sorry," he croaked.

Betty kissed his damp hair. "There's nothing for you to be sorry about."

She chattered cheerfully as she helped him into dry clothes and tucked him into bed. It was only when she'd left the room to make tea that she covered her face with her hands and wept into them as silently as she could, terror tearing her apart from the inside out.

There was no money for a doctor, not if she wanted to keep a roof over her ailing husband's head for one more week. How could she nurse him on the street? How could she nurse him on her own?

How could she save him? She *had* to save him. For to let him die was to know that he had given his life for her, had surrendered his safe, warm existence for this life of toil and hardship because he loved her, and she would not allow that to happen.

She could not.

~ ~ ~ ~ ~

Will's neck arched backward, glistening with sweat as his head drove into the pillow. A cry escaped his clenched teeth, and his arms flailed in the sweat-soaked sheets.

142

"Will! Will, my darling, it's not real," Betty cried. "It's not real."

But to Will's fevered eyes, something terrifying was in the dark room with them. Betty could not afford gas; a candle stub burned on the nightstand, filling the room with a feeble and fickle light. Will's eyes darted from shadow to shadow, his face unrecognizable with terror, his skin grey. He screamed and flailed, then curled into a ball as terrible coughs racked his body. They were so loud, so hard and violent, that Betty feared they would wrench his ribs from his spine.

She plunged her cloth into a pail of cool water at her feet and rung it out, her fingers stinging with cold. All the same, when she'd run the cloth over Will's face and arms, it was hot in her hands.

"Rest, darling, rest," she begged him. "You'll feel better if you only rest."

Will's coughs subsided, and he fell back and lay motionless except for his labouring chest as he drew in breaths that sounded agonizing and wet. His shoulders pumped with each breath, as though the muscles of his ribcage had grown too tired to expand his lungs.

Betty laid the cool cloth over his forehead and rested her hand over it. Her heart pounded painfully in her chest, and as Will slipped into a deeper sleep, she lowered her exhausted head onto her arm. Down the street, the church bell struck three in the morning, and Betty had had no sleep.

Nor would she have any. She kept her eyes wide open, watching the struggling rise and fall of Will's chest.

Too many people had already left her. Her mother. Miss Parker. Adelaide. Martha.

Will could not leave her, too, not if she could help it. The thought of losing him made the shadows grow larger, closer, ready to sink their claws into her and drag her into absolute darkness. Hot tears rolled down her cheeks, and she grasped his hand tightly, blazing hot against her palm.

"I need you, darling," she whispered. "Oh, Will, I need you."

He made no response, but he kept breathing in wet, laborious gasps.

For now.

~ ~ ~ ~ ~

Betty stood in the bedroom door, staring at the huddled form on the bed.

She'd fallen asleep somewhere around six that morning. When she jerked awake, the room was dappled with sunlight, and for a horrifying instant Betty was certain that Will was dead. But a second later she realized what had woken her; he was struggling to raise himself on the pillows, coughing and heaving violently, sounding like a drowning man.

She'd pulled him upright and held the pail as he spat horrific globs of phlegm. He had stayed awake long enough to take two sips of tea; then the fever took hold again, his eyes rolled back in his head, and he sagged beneath the covers once more.

As far as she could tell, he now slept peacefully enough, even though his shoulders still jerked and twitched with every breath. His breathing sounded worse. It rattled and wheezed; occasionally, coughs ravaged his body, ending in long groans of pain.

"I don't want to leave you, darling," Betty whispered. "But I have to find help, or—" She couldn't finish the sentence, but the appalling possibility loomed over her like a storm on the verge of breaking.

She shut the bedroom door softly, leaving a childishly scrawled note on the nightstand, and went to the kitchen table. The address book sprawled open on the table and she flipped it open to check the address one more time.

Mr. Evans, 12 Hitchcock Street.

Betty pulled on her coat and left the house, striding out briskly, her boots clopping on the swept pavement. It had not snowed in the night; the sky above was as grey and unyielding as steel, and dirty ice had formed on the cobblestones, but Betty strode on with reckless speed.

It was a stupid hope, perhaps, that this would be Mr. Bernie Evans, Martha's brother. But it was the only hope that she had left.

~ ~ ~ ~ ~

Betty had been praying under her breath for four blocks when she finally saw the sign hanging from a lamppost: *Hitchcock Street.*

Her heart thumped unpleasantly against her ribs, and not only from the exertion of walking for nearly two hours on an empty stomach. She tucked her hands into her sleeves, shivering in the cold wind that howled down the narrow street, and stared at the houses on either side.

These were much smaller than the building containing Betty's flat. Many were little more than cottages, and they were misshapen and tumbledown with cracked facades, sagging roofs, windows boarded up here and there. One had a heap of rubble instead of a chimney, and smoke bled through the hole in the roof, dark and reeking.

Most of the cottages opened directly onto the street; one or two had drooping, rotten wooden fences trying in vain to defend tiny strips of garden from the pavement.

Number 12 was one of the houses with such a fence. The gate was missing—Betty spotted it leaning against the wall, half buried in snow—and she shuffled up to the front door. It had been red once; now so much of the paint had peeled that more wood than paint was visible. The whitewashed walls were grimy, and the roof sagged beneath the weight of the snow, but a wisp of grey smoke escaped the fat little chimney. It was a Sunday, and someone had to be home.

Betty braced herself and raised her hand to knock. More paint flaked from the door at the thud of her knuckles, and she flinched back, hoping no one would notice.

Heavy footsteps thudded over the floor. The door jerked open, and a thickset man with heavy jowls that hung like a bloodhound's regarded her with bloodshot eyes. Stale beer rolled from his breath.

"What?" he hissed.

Betty plucked up her courage. *For Will,* she reminded herself. "Excuse me, sir," she said, "are you Mr. Bernard Evans?"

The man grunted.

Betty's pulse pounded in her wrist. "You are?"

"Said so, din't I?" the man snapped. "If this is about shoes, it's Sunday. I ain't doing no repairs on a Sunday."

Betty's heart leaped. Martha had mentioned once that her brother was a cobbler, although he'd lost his shop years ago and now worked at home.

"I'm not here about shoes," said Betty.

"Go away, then," Bernie growled, and went to shut the door.

"Wait!" Betty seized it, stopping him. "I'm sorry, sir. Please wait. I have to ask you something."

Bernie rolled his eyes. "What is it?"

"Do you know Martha Evans?" Betty asked breathlessly.

For a second that stretched into eternity, Bernie stared at her with his rheumy eyes. Then he grunted, "Course I know her. She's my sister."

"Oh, sir!" Betty held back tears of joy. "Do you possibly know where I could find her?"

Bernie jabbed a thumb over his shoulder. In the gloom of the cottage, Betty spotted the outline of a grey doorway etched into the wall.

"In there," he grunted. "Shut the door behind you." He turned and stumped deeper into the cottage.

Betty sprang inside, slammed the door and all but raced to that greyish outline. Before she could reach it, the door swung open, and she looked into the face she loved as a mother's.

"Martha!" she cried.

Martha's face was thin and haggard, but her eyes lit up at once, and she held out her arms. "Oh, Betty, my darling Little One!"

Then Betty was enfolded in a trembling embrace that smelled of porridge and stale bread, and she clung to Martha with all of her might, tears rolling down her cheeks. They stood there holding each other for several long minutes, as though to make up for all the embraces that they had missed over the past year, even though there would be no catching up on lost time.

~ ~ ~ ~ ~

"He's in a bad way, poor mite," said Martha, "but he'll be all right."

147

She leaned over Will and Betty's bed and tucked the quilt tightly around his motionless body. His breaths came more easily now; Betty had used her rent money to buy laudanum at the apothecary, and it already seemed to be working.

"Will the medicine be enough?" she asked nervously.

"It will let him sleep," said Martha simply. "He's young and strong, and you found help quickly. Perhaps it will help him." She stroked Will's hair away from his eyes. "Married! So much has happened in a year."

"In a month," Betty admitted. As they walked back to Betty's flat, she'd told Martha everything: the dismissal, the workhouse, Will's reappearance, their marriage and the way his father had disinherited him. None of it had surprised Martha. She was as steady as a rock, as always, firm and solid under Betty's wobbling feet.

"I'm sorry about what happened with Bromley House, but you two were always meant to be together, no matter how often I tried to keep you apart." Martha smiled. "Stopping your love would have been like trying to stop winter from coming."

The words warmed Betty's heart. Martha left the room and shut the door softly, and they went into the kitchen, where Betty scraped the bottom of the tin for tea and boiled the kettle.

"Thank you for coming, Martha," she said. "I... I didn't know what to do, or even what medicines to ask for." She blinked rapidly at the thought of what those medicines would cost.

"He'll feel a little better when he wakes up," said Martha. "Well enough that we'll be able to get him on a tram back home."

Betty stared at her. "Home?"

"Oh, Betty, darling." Martha laughed. "Did you think that I was going to leave you here, after you'd told me that you had money for rent or medicine but not for both?"

Betty simply gaped, stunned. "But what about Bernie?"

"Bernie has his part of the house." Martha looked away. "Father left everything to him, of course, because he was the boy. It's bad enough I have to rent the bedroom where I slept as a little girl, worse that it's falling down because he cares more for drink than work. I shan't let him tell me who can stay in my little rooms with me."

"You only have part of the cottage?" said Betty.

"A bedroom, and I'm allowed to cook my food in his kitchen as long as I cook for him, too." Martha shrugged. "It's good enough for now. I'm grateful I had somewhere to go after I was thrown out of Bromley House." She paused. "I went back for you, you know."

"Will told me," said Betty.

"No one knew where you'd gone, and I thought I'd lost you forever. I never believed that codswallop about you stealing." Martha smiled. "I raised a better girl than that."

"How do you pay your rent?" Betty asked. "Or buy your food?"

"Oh, I look after some of the children in the street when their parents are at work. They can hardly afford much; they pay me a pittance, and bring me rice, milk and bread for the children. I get by."

"We'll help you," said Betty quickly. "I have work. I'll get better work, and when Will's better, he'll get a job."

Martha laid a hand on her arm. "You'll have to, darling, I'm afraid. I can barely feed myself as it is. We'll all have to tighten our belts until we have good jobs. But you'll be safe with me, and we'll finally be together again." Her eyes lit up. "We may not have roast meat this Christmas, but being together is all the miracle I need."

Chapter Fourteen

Snow thundered against the window, rattling it deafeningly, a wisp of cold air slipping through the scrap of old plank that had been used to cover the hole in the glass. Betty shivered as she walked over to the fireplace, clutching three tin cups of watery tea, no milk, no sugar. The near-colourless fluid wobbled with the tremors of her hands.

"Ah, Betty, thank you," Will rasped. He extended skeletal hands from within the folds of the rug wrapped around him. Despite the fetch that he sat in their only chair, pushed up as close as possible to the meagre sticks of firewood that smouldered miserably in the hearth, Will never seemed to be warm. He grasped a cup gratefully and wrapped his hands around it to warm them.

"I'm sorry. I couldn't get the kettle to boil," said Betty. "There just wasn't enough coal in the stove, and I don't know when Bernie will be back with more."

"Not until after Boxing Day, I'm afraid," said Martha.

"How will we cook until then?" Will asked quietly.

"We won't." Martha sipped her tea. "But we still have some wood, so we can boil the kettle over the fire, and we'll just make do with bread and cheese for dinner."

Betty watched Will closely as she sat down on the hearth rug despite the creak of her bones, weary after a long day of doing laundry; Martha sat on an upturned wooden crate. Will made no comment about having bread and cheese for Christmas Eve dinner. He just clutched the tea and stared into the flames, his eyes hollow. It was as though illness had sucked the spirit out of her husband, leaving behind this pale shell, and the thought of losing him forever gnawed at Betty's heart.

Last Christmas, he'd had stuffed peacock.

"The house is so quiet without the children," said Martha. "I'm grateful you're both here to keep me company. Those little ones tire me, but they certainly keep one from feeling too lonely."

Betty laughed. "I love little Caroline. She's so friendly."

"She was terrified of me at first. Her mother left her father, did you know that?" said Martha. "He's still alive, but he beat her and the children so that she fled. Poor woman! I charge her only a penny a week; it's all she can spare."

"It's no wonder you have no money, Martha." Will said it with a smile. "Your heart is far too kind for business."

Martha chuckled. "'Better a dinner of herbs where love is than a stalled ox and hatred therewith.'"

"Is that from the Bible?" Betty asked. "I remember you reading from it when I was little."

"Proverbs," said Martha, "and never a truer word was spoken. Our Christmas dinner might be small and our home cold, but I'm glad to be here with you."

The warmth in her eyes and voice were real, but Betty pulled her coat more closely around her shoulders and struggled to feel the same. Her hunger was real, too, and it clawed at the inside of her belly. Even worse was the guilt as she watched Will sip his tea, his hands bluish and bony as he clutched his mug, trembling with weakness.

"I still can't believe what Olive did with that comb." Martha shook her head. "Jealous little minx! She could have destroyed poor Betty's life. She wasted a whole year in a workhouse as it is."

"Well, not quite wasted, Martha." Betty raised her head. "I met the governess who left me in the marketplace."

Martha straightened. "What! You did?"

"Yes. She asked me forgiveness on her deathbed and told me everything," said Betty. "She recognized me because I look so much like my grandmother."

"Did you find out who your family is?" Martha cried.

Betty shook her head. "She died before she could tell me their names." She still believed it was a last act of hatred from Miss Parker that she had never said the names. "I'll never be able to find them, but at least now I know why she left me."

"Why would anyone do such a thing?" said Martha.

"She had an affair with my father, and when my mother found out, Miss Parker decided to abandon me in a marketplace out of spite," said Betty.

Suddenly, all colour drained from Martha's face. The tin cup tumbled from her hands and clattered loudly on the hearth stones.

"Martha!" Will jumped to her feet. "Are you all right?"

"She's going to faint!" Betty yelped.

Will fanned Martha with the corner of his rug as Betty rushed to her side and loosened her corset strings. Martha gasped for air, her face ashen, hands clutching at her wooden crate.

"What's wrong?" Betty cried, panicking.

Martha seized Betty's arm. "The governess. Miss Parker," she rasped. "Was her married name Brooks? Rose Brooks?"

Betty swallowed hard. "Yes."

Martha was shaking uncontrollably. "Betty, I think I know who your birth mother is."

This time it was Betty's knees that buckled. They thudded on the floor as she fell onto them. "What?"

"Fifteen years ago, I worked at another townhouse in London, not far from there." Martha raised her eyes to Betty's. "It belonged to Mr. and Mrs. Wilkes. They had a little daughter, a baby. I had just moved to London and I was only there for a few months before Mrs. Bromley attended a gala dinner there and offered me a better wage because she so loved my cooking. I left long before the little girl was old enough for a governess, but I knew two things; that Mr. Wilkes had a wandering eye, and that Mrs. Wilkes loved that baby more than anything in the world."

Betty held her breath. Will's eyes were as big and round as saucers.

"I had been working at Bromley House for years—you were seven or eight—when I heard about what happened to the Wilkes's. We had just hired a new housemaid and she was a terrible gossip. You know how Franny could gossip."

Betty nodded.

"Well, she told me how Carol Wilkes' little girl was taken from her and abandoned. They always suspected it was the governess, but could never find her, so it was impossible to prove. They also managed to keep the abandonment out of the papers." Martha gulped. "They were not so lucky when it came to the affair. Franny told me about the child being abandoned—the public story was that the girl had died—but word of the

154

affair got out that year. It was all over the papers, and Mr. Wilkes was all but ruined. He had to turn to foreign investors to keep his business from going under completely. I never cared for talk of affairs, but I remember thinking that the governess must have abandoned the child because she was angry with Mr. Wilkes. I remember the way he stared at me through the kitchen window. He was the type of man who could charm a woman and then break her heart."

Betty's heart pounded in her throat. "Do you believe that...that I could be Mr. Wilkes' daughter?"

"I do." Martha smoothed down her hair with trembling hands. "I always thought that your governess must have abandoned you on orders from your mother or father, perhaps because you were illegitimate, or one girl too many for a husband seeking a baby boy. Parents do all kinds of horrible things to their children. But if the governess knew you... if she admitted that that was why you were abandoned... well, the story is simply too similar to the story of the Wilkes to be a coincidence."

Betty grabbed Martha's arm. "Mrs. Brooks said that I looked just like my grandmother. Do you remember what Mrs. Wilkes' mother looked like?"

"I don't," said Martha. "I never met her; she was convalescing from an illness in Spain the year that I worked there."

"Then how will we ever find out the truth?" Betty cried.

Silence hung in the room for a few long minutes.

"We will have to go to the Wilkes's' house," said Will.

"Are you mad?" Betty cried.

"No, he isn't. Not mad at all," said Martha. "I know the way there. Mr. Wilkes died a few years ago, but Mrs. Wilkes is still living there. If anyone will know you by your resemblance to your grandmother, it's her."

"What if she sets her dogs on us? What if she chases us away?" Betty cried. "What if she won't let us stay with her?"

"It's not about staying with her, Betty," said Will gently, wrapping his hands around hers. "It's not about her big home or her money. It's about you."

Betty met his eyes. They were still reddened, but their Christmas tree green glowed brighter than ever.

"It's about allowing you to know your own mother," Will whispered. "The one who loved you more than anything."

Tears filled Betty's eyes, and she bowed her head, allowing him to kiss her forehead with aching tenderness.

"We'll go in the morning," said Martha firmly.

No one argued.

~ ~ ~ ~ ~

It was a merciful thing that the tram line took them as close as a single block from Snowfall Abbey, for Will could barely walk that distance. He leaned heavily on a stick in one hand, his free arm draped over Betty's shoulders, and they laboured up the hill toward the great house.

"We should have left you at home," Betty fretted.

"I wasn't going to let you do this alone," Will panted. "I'm all right."

Betty dreaded the thought of the long walk back down the hill in humiliation, of the fee to take the tram back to their cottage, money that was meant to buy food for a pitiful Christmas dinner. At this rate, they would have nothing more than gruel.

She did not permit herself to consider, even for a moment, that Mrs. Wilkes really was her mother. She crushed that hope brutally; the disappointment, if she allowed it, would kill her.

Music poured from the huge houses they passed, Christmas carols sung by the warm and well-fed as they awaited a delicious lunch. Betty tried not to listen to them, thinking how much easier it was to believe in herald angels when one stood before a crackling fire, but she was praying all the same as they reached the great wrought-iron gates of the old abbey. The building was enormous, even bigger than Bromley House, a great square with arched windows and Gothic columns and gargoyles creeping over the eaves.

"This is madness," Betty muttered.

"Come!" said Martha, tugging the gates open a fraction.

"Martha!" cried Betty. "We should go around to the servants' entrance."

"You're coming here as her daughter, Betty, if what we believe is right and if the glory of Providence has brought us here to this moment," said Martha firmly. "Daughters use the front door."

Betty and Will trailed behind as Martha marched up the long drive and hammered on the great double doors at the front of the abbey. They caught up just as those doors swung open, revealing an elegant butler in top hat and tails.

"Sir—" said Martha.

"Begone, you vagabonds," said the butler. "Can you not see that this is the main entrance? Go, and seek trouble elsewhere!"

"We're not seeking trouble, sir!" said Martha. "We've come to—"

The butler pointed imperiously. "Go!"

"Mr. Gants," said a soft voice from inside, "who is at the door?"

The butler gave Martha a glare. "Nobody, Mrs. Wilkes. Only some foolish beggars who found the wrong entrance."

"It is so bitterly cold, Mr. Gants," said the tender voice. "Let us tell them the way around to the servants' entrance, and have the cook give them some bread."

"We are not beggars!" said Martha loudly. "My name is Martha Evans, and I was your cook once, and I have something very important to tell you."

Betty cowered behind Martha as soft footsteps came to the door.

"Ma'am, please," said the butler.

"I remember Martha," said the soft voice. "She was a good woman; if she has something to tell me, let her tell me."

Tears stung Betty's eyes. Surely this was not possible. Surely, if her mother was a rich woman, she could not be kind and lovely and trusting as well. It was too much; it was wildly beyond what she could dare to hope for.

Perhaps, though, it was only almost as wild and unbelievable as the thought that God would become man and be born in a grubby manger to save the world from its sins, and not only that, but that He would also fill the world with Christmas lights and gifts and carols and men with pine-green eyes and gentle hands.

The woman who came to the door had a face lined with both worry and smiles. Her eyes were bright blue, her face only minimally powdered, and she wore a dress of the deepest Christmas red, trimmed with gold. Warm light poured from the room behind her, silhouetting her, like a halo.

"Martha, it's good to see you," said Mrs. Wilkes. "Do you still work for the Bromley's?"

"Never mind me, ma'am," said Martha. "There's someone I'd like you to meet."

She grabbed Betty's arm and propelled her forward, and Mrs. Wilkes' eyes found hers. Instant recognition flooded her face. She reeled back a step, pressing both hands to her mouth, and her breaths came in what could have been either sobs or laughter. Betty froze, her veins feeling as though they'd been filled suddenly with falling snow instead of blood.

"Mrs. Wilkes!" The butler grasped her arm. "Are you all right?"

"All right? *All right*? Oh, Mr. Gants," said Mrs. Wilkes faintly, "I may be better than I have been in twelve long years." She pulled away from him and stepped toward Betty, her fingertips brushing over Betty's face, the touch warm and tender. "You look just like my mother," she whispered.

"Mrs. Wilkes, I—" Betty swallowed. "I was abandoned in a marketplace by my governess, Miss Parker, twelve Christmases ago, when I was five."

Tears filled Mrs. Wilkes' eyes.

Mr. Gants stepped back, a gloved hand raised to his mouth. "We never told the press the name of the governess," he said faintly. "We never told anyone."

"Oh, Mr. Gants," said Mrs. Wilkes, "as if we needed any confirmation. As if her resemblance was not proof enough that my daughter, my beautiful baby girl, has finally come home to me. Betty, my Betty, you don't know how I've missed you for every moment that you've been gone!"

She flung her arms wide open, and Betty's tears rolled down to mingle with her laughter as she walked into her mother's arms at last.

Epilogue

Six Years Later

The fat kitten tumbled among discarded ribbons and scraps of brown paper thrown aside in wild excitement. It was pure white, a blue ribbon tied around its little neck, and it batted happily at bits of ribbon in the chaos on the drawing-room carpet.

Betty rose from her seat on the chaise-longue and scooped the kitten out of the way seconds before a pair of stockinged little feet descended where the little animal had been.

"Careful, Addie!" she said, laughing. "You almost squashed Snowball."

The little girl was three, and she had dancing blue eyes like both of her grandmothers. She giggled, hugging a beautiful new doll to her chest, the fine porcelain of its face hardly more perfect than the child's soft skin. "Sorry, Mama."

"It's all right, my darling," said Betty.

She settled the kitten in her lap, where he licked his fur contentedly. Will wrapped an arm around her shoulders and tickled the kitten's cheek with his free hand.

Addie bounced across the floor to the armchair where Carol Wilkes, her grandmother, sat watching the scene with a benevolent smile. "Play a song for us, Grandmama!"

Carol laughed. "Which song?"

"O Christmas Tree," said Addie. "My favourite." She tilted back her head to gaze at the magnificent tree that towered in a corner of the vast room, draped in glittering finery, an angel glowing at the top. The angel was tattered and tired, but when Carol's eyes followed Addie's to it, they still lit up with an old fondness.

"Oh, all right," she said. "O Christmas Tree it is!"

She rose to her feet and strolled to the grand piano in a corner of the room. Addie toddled after her. With a rhythmic thudding of wooden rockers on the carpet, Betty's older daughter followed, giggling gleefully as she straddled her latest Christmas gift: a rocking-horse wrapped in brown velveteen, with real horsehair for the mane and tail, her fingers gripping the red leather reins.

Carol took her time composing herself on the stool and rifling through her songbook. Martha came in while the girls watched their grandmother with rapt attention. She carried a silver tray on which rested cups of hot chocolate, rich and ready to fend off the cold of the snow glittering outside the big window.

"Thank you, Martha." Will rose and took the tray from her. "Please be careful of those hands."

"Don't you worry, Master Will," said Martha, smiling.

Will blushed, still unused to being called that even after six years as the heir to Snowfall Abbey.

"My hands are doing quite all right with the work of a nurse instead of a cook." Martha's love shone in her eyes. "Nurse to the two loveliest little girls in the world. Our little ones."

Martha had refrained from calling Betty her Little One after Betty was re-united with her mother, but Caroline Wilkes had taken to Martha with the deepest gratitude. "Betty has two mothers. Don't you ever forget that Martha. Who knows what terrible things might have befallen her, if it weren't for you. She will always belong to both of us. She is *our* Little One." Martha had wiped the tears from her old eyes that day. It was a rare sight.

Betty sighed with pleasure. "Oh, you're so right, Martha. Our Little Ones are perfect gifts."

Martha watched as they tugged Carol's skirt and giggled while she arranged her songbook on the piano. "Did you see the bit in the paper about Mr. Bromley?"

"Yes." Will laid a hand on Betty's knee. "This might sound dreadful, Martha, but I'm relieved that he's gone. Not only does it bring me peace, but perhaps now he, too, will have peace at last."

"I hear that his faith changed while he was an invalid," said Martha. "I hope you're right." She chuckled. "But why talk about such things on a day like this? Play the hymn, Mrs. Wilkes!"

Carol chuckled and played the first few bars, and the two girls danced around the piano, giggling.

Betty took Will's hand. "Does it ever bother you?" she asked softly.

"What?" Will asked.

"That your younger brother has inherited your father's entire estate—him and Olive," said Betty.

Will shook his head. "It neither surprised nor upset me when Olive married him," he said. "As for the estate..." He spread his arms, gesturing at the wonderful tree and the children, the hot chocolate, the kitten and the laughter that filled the room.

"I have everything I need right here. This family is the greatest Christmas gift I could ever have imagined."

Betty leaned her head on his shoulder as the carol filled the air. When her mother began to sing, Betty joined in with all of her heart.

A symbol of goodwill and love
You'll ever be unchanging!

THE END

Thank you for reading my book
I hope that you enjoyed it!

Over the page you will find a preview of another of my
books.

Preview

The Waif's Lost Family

Chapter One

The cotton mill echoed with cacophonous sound, but none of it came from the toiling figures of the men, women and children who laboured within its dark and dusty belly. Everything in the mill seemed to be contributing to the din except for them: the roaring steam engine that drove the machines, the hiss of yarn spinning on the billies, the clatter and thump of the mule, the clack and judder of the looms. Among the chaos of noise, the people working inside seemed like insignificant ants, crawling miserably across the face of the heartless industry. And above everything hung a pall of dust,

barely broken by the bits of light that came in through the high windows, fading rapidly as the sun began to set and ineffectively replaced by dusty gas lamps that burned like fevered eyes in the choking darkness.

Gwen Hopewell knew very well why everyone inside the cotton mill was so utterly silent. There was neither time, nor breath, nor energy left for talking. Everyone in the mill was toiling just as hard as she was, even her little sister, Roberta. It hardly seemed fair that Roberta should be here beside her, hastening up and down the length of the billy as what seemed like a hundred lengths of white yarn spun upon it. She was only ten years old, and her pale little face was already pinched with exhaustion, even though it was only six o' clock; there were still hours of work waiting for them. Roberta's blue eyes were bloodshot as they scanned up and down the rows of threads, searching for any imperfection.

There was so much that Gwen wanted to do for Roberta. She wanted to give her a word of encouragement, or to help her somehow, or even just to stop and wrap her in an embrace, as if that would do her aching little body any good. But Gwen was only twelve herself, and there was no time to stop, no breath to speak. Dust had been choking her lungs all day, and she kept wiping her nose on a tattered sleeve as she hurried up and down her end of the billy, waiting for a thread to snap.

It was impossible to hear the yarn when it broke. Everything was just too loud. But Gwen's eyes, strained as they were by a full day of keeping her gaze locked steadily on the yarn, instantly picked out the flying end of a broken piece. She broke into a jog, hurrying to grab the broken end. The wheel was spinning frantically; machinery clicked and snapped dangerously under her fingers like a rabid dog. Her fingers were aching from the work, and the yarn

burned her skin, but she found the other end and tied it in a brisk, quick movement.

The yarn sprung tight in her hands, and Gwen let go, stepping back. The billy went on working, the yarn went on spinning, and Gwen allowed herself a short breath of relief.

"Gwen?"

Roberta's voice sounded quiet, but Gwen knew she was shouting at the top of her voice just to make herself heard. She turned, forcing a smile for her sister's sake. "What is it?" she yelled.

Roberta dragged a filthy hand over her brow, smearing sweat and dirt together. "I'm thirsty," she shouted.

Gwen's heart felt like it was being trampled. "We'll get a water break soon," she bellowed back. Roberta gave her the long, silent look of a child who knew she was being lied to.

There were so few water breaks, and the air was so dry...

Then Gwen saw it: the white end of a broken piece of yarn, flapping hopelessly on the far side of the billy, where Roberta was supposed to be watching it.

"Bobbie!" she gasped, more terrified than exasperated. She shoved past her sister and ran to the broken thread, but her hands were already sweaty with fear. The yarn slipped through her fingers, burning her skin, and she had to grab at it twice before she could finally tie it off –

"OI!" thundered a masculine voice. "YOU!"

Gwen whipped around. A heavyset man with a week's greasy beard was lumbering among the machinery towards her, a grubby cigarette dangling from the corner of his mouth. That cigarette seemed to be permanently part of him; its cheap smoke had long since stained his dirty, overlong fingernails a

nasty shade of yellow, which matched his jaundiced eyes as they fixed upon Gwen.

Her heart thudded painfully in her chest. Wherever their supervisor went, people dropped their eyes to the ground, their shoulders hunching in simple fear.

Hugh Worley leaned on a walking stick as he came up to Gwen, still sucking on the ever-present cigarette. It wobbled in his mouth as he spoke.

"What's the matter with you?" he snarled, his lips flapping loose and fleshy over each syllable. "You let that thread stay broken for far too long." He lifted the stick and held it across his body, slapping it into his free palm with a meaty thud.

Gwen knew the feel of that walking stick, and she couldn't take her eyes off it. Behind her, she could hear Roberta whimpering with fear. A flare of anger rose in her. She wasn't the one who had been neglecting her threads.

"This is your fault," she muttered.

"What was that?" shouted Worley, leaning a little closer so that his sweaty, smoky odour could be added to the general stench of the cotton mill.

Gwen took a deep breath. As always, she knew what she had to do.

"It was my fault, sir!" she shouted. "I wasn't looking!"

A dangerous gleam filled Worley's small, angry eyes. He raised the stick. "Hold out your hand," he ordered.

Gwen's eyes prickled with tears. At least the beating was better than having her wages docked. She did so, holding out her left hand, and screwed her eyes tightly shut.

"Now don't move," snapped Worley.

Gwen didn't dare. To flinch away was to incur an extra blow. There was a whistling sound, and the

stick thumped down across Gwen's palm with a burning pain. She forced herself to stay still, keeping her flinches to her shoulders and hips as the stick thumped home over and over again until her palm went from stinging to burning to aching to numb.

Worley was out of breath when he stopped. Sweat dribbled down his filthy face as he glared at her. "Now get back to work," he spat. "Don't make me take away your wages."

"Yes, sir. I will, sir," Gwen gasped through her tears.

Worley strode away, and Gwen turned back to her work, letting the tears fall unchecked down her cheeks. She felt a

fluttering touch on her arm and glanced down to see Roberta looking up at her, her eyes brimming with tears.

"I'm so sorry," Roberta said.

Gwen turned away. "I'm not angry," she said, and it was the truth. "Let's just get back to work."

Work: ultimately, that was all that their lives had become.

~ ~ ~ ~ ~

There had been a slightly better time once, but Gwen never spoke of it. She didn't want Roberta to know that their lives used to be better. She didn't want Roberta to grieve a better life the way she was doing right now.

The walk home was not a long one, but for Gwen, it was always the most miserable part of her day. It was very dark by the time they left the ugly, looming building of the cotton mill behind and turned their steps towards the housing – if it could be called that – that gave mill workers somewhere to live in the

nearby suburbs. At least in the early mornings, Gwen had a little strength, even if it was very dark. But now, her legs were trembling from exhaustion, her feet aching steadily. And there

was a throbbing pain in her palm from the beating it had taken by Worley.

Keeping Roberta's small hand firmly clutched in her uninjured hand, Gwen tried to think of something else as she walked back towards home. Sometimes, like today, her mind wandered unchecked back to that other time. They had lived in a tenement then too, but at least they hadn't shared it with another family. In fact, they'd had two sleeping pallets: one for her and Roberta, and another one for Mama and Papa. Food had been scarce, but they never went a day without eating. And there had been laughter in their home at times.

That had all been before Papa died trying to save a little scavenger from under one of the cotton mill's cruel machines. He had barely been buried when Gwen, only six at the time, was sent to work in the very same mill.

She pushed the thoughts aside and forced a smile for Roberta. "Nearly home, love," she said, giving her sister a little tug to encourage her to keep up.

"My feet are so tired," Roberta complained.

"I know. I know." Gwen sighed. "But it's not far. Come on now."

She tried to keep her eyes straight forward as they entered the slum. All around them, a scene of utter despair and squalor rolled past, every block worse than the one preceding it. Row after row of houses with thin walls, broken windows and rattling roofs watched them pass like silent beggars ignored on street corners, their fading paint and empty window-frames crying out silently for help and attention. The paving had long since given way to mud, which sucked at Gwen's tired feet and seeped through the gaps in her shoes so that her socks turned slowly cold and sticky.

Around her, a drove of people, faceless, voiceless, the very life sucked out of them by their day at the mill, were journeying towards their insufficient homes and meagre suppers just as she was. Their faces were hidden by the darkness, broken only intermittently by old streetlamps lit with flickering, sickly flames.

All of the people moved with the same broken desperation as Gwen did; driven home only by the knowledge that there might be rest there, their toiling, aching bodies barely capable of the final effort of walking home. Yet even these were better off than the few figures that Gwen saw huddled in nooks and crannies, alleyways and odd corners. She tried her best not to look at them, but sometimes the horrors dragged her eyes unbidden from her path. An old woman, lying on her side, stretched out on the mud, looking stone dead except for the odd breath that lifted her old chest and stirred the lock of muddy grey hair hanging over her face.

A young man, leaning against the wall of an alley, staring down at the hem of his tattered shirt, pulling off bits of thread that were fraying loose and tucking carefully into his pocket as if there was some use left in them. A young woman lay curled beside him, a baby in her arms. The baby was crying, a thin, weak, monotonous wail; the woman did not wake, and the man did not spare it a second glance.

As Gwen passed by, she saw that the woman had a suppurating wound on her elbow where it pressed into the filthy street.

She shuddered, tucking an arm around Roberta's shoulders and turning her away so that she wouldn't see the horrifying sight. "Nearly home, Bobbie," she said, trying to make her voice as cheerful as possible. "Tomorrow's Sunday, too, so we don't have to go to work. And I'm sure there's still a little piece of that salt fish for dinner. You and Teddy can share it."

Roberta cheered up a little. "Yes, there is!" she said. "But why should Teddy have any? He's just been sitting at home all day." She frowned. "And he's six years old already. He should be working, just like I was, at his age."

Gwen knew, because it was the same age that she, too, had been sent to the cotton mill when their father had died. Being a scavenger – crawling under those great, clanking, deadly machines to clean them while they were running – was dangerous and horrible work, but nothing could ever be more horrible than watching her tiny sister do it.

There had been times when Roberta had cried through an entire sixteen-hour shift, the tears washing twin trails of clean skin through the grubbiness of her face.

Yet even that could never be worse than what had happened to Joey.

"You know why Mama won't send him to the cotton mill, Bobbie," said Gwen, dragging her mind away from the awful memory; the blood, the screams... and then the silence.

"But she sent us," said Roberta.

"That was before Joey," said Gwen.

Silence fell between them, the way it always did any time Joey's name was mentioned. Roberta gave Gwen a sheepish look. "I'm sorry," she said. "I didn't mean..."

"I know," said Gwen.

"I'm just hungry. And I think Teddy should be pulling his weight some way or another."

"Never mind that now," said Gwen. "Look – we're home."

They turned left into the doorway of one of the many buildings that all looked the same. Roberta pushed the door open as Gwen cast a glance up to the third window on the right, their window. It was boarded up, and there was no sound from inside.

They walked into a dinghy hallway and followed a set of stairs that crackled ominously under their feet until they reached the third floor and their tenement. Gwen laid a hand on the door; there was no knob or latch, just a piece of worn string that hooked around a nail. She took a deep breath, trying to steel herself for another evening at home, and pushed the door open.

The interior was a mess of hopeless squalor. With the window boarded up, only chinks of light from the streetlamp outside could even hope to enter the room.

After the vastness of the cotton mill, the room was puny – but its atmosphere no less stifling, thick with the odour of unwashed humanity. A single candle guttered on an upturned bucket on the floor. Together with the light from measly fire that spluttered miserably in the single hearth, the candle illuminated the small room, which served as two family homes.

Nearest to the door, there were two sleeping pallets; one contained a tousle-haired mass of hungry, bony children, who slept the sleep of the sick under a piece of sacking for a blanket. Their mother perched on the edge of the pallet beside them.

On the other pallet, an enormous, hairy, shirtless man lay supine, his bearded chin pointing towards the roof, the tangle of his chest hair no less dark and meaningless than the mass of lines on his forehead. His eyes were closed, but his wife watched him as though he might explode at any moment.

Gwen knew why. Mr. Brown had a nasty temper when he had been drinking, and he had always been drinking. She could smell the stale reek of old alcohol rolling off his breath as he slept, and she tiptoed across the floor, avoiding Mrs. Brown's eyes.

Stepping around Mr. Brown's disgustingly hairy bare feet, Gwen reached for the thin, grubby curtain that separated her home from the Brown's'. She held it aside as Roberta slipped through the gap, then followed it into the tiny area that the Hopewell family called home. Here, there was no hearth, and just a single narrow sleeping pallet pushed up against the wall.

There was about four square feet of floor space in all, and Gwen's little brother was sitting on it, playing contentedly with a broken matchstick and a piece of string. He dropped them both as he looked up, and his dirty little face lit up. "Gwen! Bobbie!" he whispered, hurrying over to them and throwing his arms around Gwen's knees.

Gwen felt everything inside her melting. She crouched down and wrapped her arms around Teddy. "Hello, love," she whispered.

"Hush," said a reedy voice from the sleeping pallet. "Mr. Brown is asleep."

Gwen looked up. Her mother, bone-thin, sat on the pallet, a half-finished slop-shop jacket draped across her knees. She was sewing it with trembling fingers, not looking up from her work when Roberta and Gwen came in. Her legs were stretched out on the pallet, bare feet exposed beneath her fraying skirt. Even though it had been years since Mama had last worked in the factory, Gwen was still always startled by the sight of her legs.

Even though Mama's feet lay several inches apart on the pallet, her shins tapered sharply towards one another. Under her skirt, Gwen knew that Mama's knees were touching. They had given in after decades of standing in the cotton mill and not eating enough. Like Gwen, Mama had started as a scavenger when she was only six.

The mill had taken everything from her, even Joey. Gwen reminded herself of this when Mama's tone scalded her weary heart.

"Don't worry, Mama." She forced a smile. "We'll be very quiet."

"Very quiet," echoed Teddy, turning his great, blue eyes up towards Gwen.

She smiled down at him, more easily this time. "I brought some bread for supper," she said. "And there's salt fish for you and Bobbie, Teddy."

At this, Mama finally set aside her work and looked up. "Isn't there enough for you to have some too, Gwen?" she asked.

"Oh, no thank you, Mama," said Gwen. "I don't need it."

Mama's eyes dwelt on her for a long moment, softening. "Come here, love," she said, holding out an arm. "Bobbie, get the bread – we'll eat together."

Gwen went eagerly to her mother's side. She sat down on the pallet, feeling the hard wooden slats on her thighs, and Mama pulled her into a gentle embrace.

"My children, my children," she sighed. "What in this world would I do without you?"

Gwen buried her face in Mama's neck. "You don't have to be without us, Mama," she said. "I promise."

Mama hugged her tighter, trembling. Gwen knew she was thinking of Joey.

The screams filled her mind again, and she pushed them away. She could never let that happen to her family again.

~ ~ ~ ~ ~

Sunday flitted by much too quickly. It was spent the way Gwen and Roberta spent nearly every Sunday; curled upside by side on the sleeping pallet, finally claiming the sleep that their bodies had been craving all week long. Besides, if they slept through most of the day, then they wouldn't realize how hungry they were. Occasionally, Gwen had half woken to hear Teddy playing too loudly or asking Mama when there would be something to eat again, but Mama would always hush him quickly, and Gwen could drift back to sleep.

By contrast, as usual, Monday's shift at the mill seemed a thousand hours long. Gwen's hand still ached from the beating it had taken from Worley, and piecing was a constant battle. At least this time, Roberta had kept her eyes on her threads, not letting them break on her watch like she had done on Saturday.

Still, Gwen felt as exhausted as though she had never had a day off in the six years since she had started working at the cotton mill. She plodded up the wobbly stairs of their tenement with her head held low, interested only in food and sleep. Roberta was close on her heels, clutching all the food that they could buy with their meagre earnings on a Monday; the rent had been paid that morning, but by tomorrow they would already have to start setting most of their wages aside to pay the rent again the following week.

Tired though she was, the moment Gwen pushed the door open and stepped into the Brown's half of the tenement, she knew instantly that something was terribly amiss.

Mr. Brown wasn't home.

She stared. The room seemed bigger without his presence, yet his absence had failed to abate Mrs. Brown's fear. She was sitting on her pallet, hugging her children to her and weeping, a steady, mournful wail that seemed to be wearing thin from constant crying. Gwen stared at her, then glanced at Roberta, who shrugged. Part of her urged her to reach out and wrap her arms around the young mother and her starving little children, but she did not have the strength.

She turned away instead and pushed through the curtain, and that was where things were even more wrong.

Teddy was sitting in a corner, clutching his knees to his chest, his eyes the only clean and white things in the entire tenement; they were very wide and round with fear.

And Mama wasn't working. Unlike Roberta and Gwen, Mama didn't have Sundays; she had to work constantly in order to meet the ridiculous quotas that the slop-shop gave her. Gwen couldn't remember the last time she'd seen her mother doing anything other than working or sleeping or eating,

but right now, Mama wasn't doing any of those things. She was just… sitting. Her eyes were wide too, and she was staring into the middle distance, her face utterly ashen under its usual layer of grime.

If Teddy had not been sitting there, alive and well, Gwen would have feared the worst. Mama looked the way she did when Gwen had come home to tell her about…

No! Gwen couldn't allow herself to think Joey's name, not now. "Mama?" she gasped, the word coming out small and trembling.

Mama blinked. She looked up at Gwen, her eyes only half focused. "Children," she croaked, forcing something like a smile.

"What's the matter, Mama?" Roberta went over to her and sat down on the edge of the pallet, a few feet from Mama, as if fearful that she might break her if she touched her. "Is it your legs again?"

"No, no, darling." Mama paused, wrestling with tears. "It's… it's…"

"Please." Gwen fell to her knees on the end of the pallet. "Please, Mama, what's going on?"

"Where's Mr. Brown?" asked Roberta.

"He's left," said Mama.

There was a beat of silence. Gwen didn't understand. "But why does Mrs. Brown look so worried?" she asked. "Normally she's glad when he's gone, even if he comes home so drunk and angry."

"You don't understand, Gwendoline." Mama's tone grew harsh, and she looked up at Gwen with burning eyes. "He's left her. He's gone. He's not coming back. She's going to be on her own now with those little ones…" Her voice broke, and she dropped her gaze to her lap again.

"What will she do?" asked Roberta.

"What we all do, Bobbie." Mama swallowed. "Whatever we have to do, to keep our children safe." She looked up at them again and this time there were tears trembling in her eyes. "I have terrible news."

"What is it?" asked Gwen.

"The rent..." Mama took a shaky breath. "The landlord has raised it. It's one and a half times what it used to be."

"No!" Gwen felt as though she'd just received a kick in the stomach.

"How?" cried Roberta, jumping to her feet. "How could he do that?"

"It's his building," said Mama. "He can do as he pleases."

"But he must know that the mill hasn't increased our wages in years," said Roberta. "How are we to survive, Mama?"

Gwen stared at her mother, desperate for an answer. But the iron resolve that had filled Mama's voice only a moment earlier seemed to be gone now. Her features crumpled, and tears started pouring down her cheeks.

"I don't know, Bobbie," she wept. "I don't know. I just don't know what to do. I don't know what we are going to do."

Gwen felt as though her innards had transformed to ice. She realized that her hands were shaking, and she interlaced her fingers, staring down at them. Mama was shattered. There was nothing left in her, and Roberta was staring at her with tears trickling down her cheeks.

"What are we going to do, Gwen?" asked a soft voice by Gwen's knees.

She looked down. Teddy had gripped her dress in both of his little fists, and he stared up at her, his eyes wide.

"I don't want to be homeless," whispered Roberta, turning to Gwen. "Winter is coming. We'll die out there."

Gwen thought of the homeless people they saw every day as they walked home from work, and everything inside her

quailed. She knew they couldn't survive – Mama with her knock knees, tiny Teddy...

There was only one thing she could think of. She bent down and put her hands on Teddy's shoulders. "Teddy, my love," she said, "you'll have to start working."

"No!" Mama's shout was louder than Gwen had expected. She shot to her feet, wobbling on her crooked legs, and seized

Teddy as if Gwen had hurt him. Hugging the child to her chest, she stared at Gwen with bloodshot, teary eyes. "My boy won't go to that awful place. He won't. He won't!"

"Mama, would you rather we starved?" cried Gwen. "We're starving as it is."

"I would rather starve than see him die as Joey did," spat Mama.

"I would care for him," said Gwen. "I'd watch him, like I did with Bobbie."

"And like you did with Joey?" Mama snapped.

Gwen took a step back as though she had been physically struck. Sensing her pain, Mama set down Teddy at once, reaching towards Gwen. "Darling, I'm sorry. I didn't mean it. I…"

"No," said Gwen, pulling back from Mama's attempt at an embrace. "You're right. I should have watched Joey." She took a deep breath. "But it's true that we won't survive if we don't get more money, Mama."

"Teddy has to do *something*," said Roberta.

"I will, I will," said Teddy, clutching at Mama's skirt. "I'll help, Mama, let me help."

"But don't send him to the cotton mill," said Gwen, exhaustion and fear tugging at every word. "Let him beg. Look at him. He would be a wonderful beggar."

Mama and Gwen both stared down at Teddy. He gazed back with his guileless blue eyes, set in a pale face surrounded by angelic golden curls.

"You're right," said Mama softly. "Oh, Teddy." She crouched down with an effort, grunting with pain as her faltering knees trembled, and wrapped the child in her arms. "I didn't want to let you go," she whispered. "But I have no choice now. I can't bear for you to leave this tenement every day, but neither can I bear to see you hungry on the streets."

"I'll be all right, Mama," said Teddy, with innocent optimism. "Gwen will show me what to do."

Mama looked up at Gwen with tears standing in her eyes. "Please," she whispered. "Take care of him, Gwen."

Gwen swallowed hard against the ache in her chest. "I promise," she said.

She had made that promise once before. But this time she was even more determined to keep it.

https://www.amazon.co.uk/Waifs-Lost-Family-Iris-Cole/dp/B0CGYYB8C5

List of Books
The Little-One's Christmas Dream
The Waif's Lost Family
The Pickpocket Orphans
The Workhouse Girls Despair
The Forgotten Match Girl's Christmas Birthday
The Wretched Needle Worker
The Lost Daughter

Would you like a FREE Book?

Join Iris Coles Newsletter

The Christmas Pauper

https://dl.bookfunnel.com/kji81fn0dr

Printed in Great Britain
by Amazon